Beautiful Surrender

by

Priscilla West

Table of Contents

Chapter Two

Chapter Three

Chapter Four

Chapter Five

Chapter Six

Chapter Seven

Chapter Eight

Chapter Nine

Chapter Ten

Chapter Eleven

Chapter Twelve

Chapter Thirteen

Epilogue

Chapter One

It was my first day of class for Econ 102. Junior year. I'd made it this far, busting my ass semester after semester, camping out in office hours, staying up late nights, living off of caffeine. Somehow I'd survived.

I thought getting into Harvard was the hard part and the rest was grade inflation, but the classes were actually pretty tough. Of course, others cruised by on raw intelligence and superhuman brains that soaked up lectures like a sponge soaking up water. Unfortunately, I couldn't do that. I was the exception. Which meant I spent my first two years making closer friends with textbooks than I did with real people.

The lecture room was large enough to fit two hundred students and it was nearly packed. Among the sea of bodies, one caught my eye. Actually, one caught the eyes of the majority of the females in the room: bright blue irises, tousled brown hair, high cheek bones, and chic glasses sitting atop a sharp nose. He looked like a male model from a J.Crew catalog except he wasn't digitally enhanced—he was real. His features were sculpted with precision and economy. Fitting. Considering the subject matter of the class—and considering he was seated in the front row, which meant he was the teacher's assistant.

I took a seat in one of the middle rows and waited for the professor to start the lecture. I could already tell this was going to be my favorite class of the semester.

***

"You know, out of over a hundred students, you're probably the only one who comes to my office hours regularly," he said with a heart-stopping smile.

I'd found out his name was Martin Pritchard. A senior economics major. Brilliant, insightful, and devilishly good-looking. It took an extraordinary amount of willpower not to get distracted by those vivid blue eyes that somehow seemed to burn hot with intensity and cold with calculation at the same time. A lot of girls had come to Martin's office hours during the beginning of the course in hopes of snagging a lay. They giggled, flitted their hair, and batted their eyes. Once they realized he was only there for academic concerns—not sexual ones—they lost interest.

He was sitting across from me in the TA office, trying to help me understand the latest assigned readings. Just the two of us.

I blushed and looked down at my notebook filled with scribbles about minimum wage laws and Nash equilibriums. I had no idea what any of it meant.

"I need the extra help. This stuff is kind of hard for me."

"You ask great questions. Ones I'd expect to hear from students from the more advanced econ classes." He grinned a perfect set of teeth. "I think you're just detailed in your thinking. Learning is a lot like putting together a puzzle. And different people have different sets of pieces. The ones with more pieces take more time to put it together, but once they do, it's a bigger picture."

I smiled bashfully, averting my gaze to my notes then returning it to him. "Thanks. I never thought of it that way."

He tapped his head. "Big picture."

We both chuckled then smiled at one another. It was definitely a shared moment and I didn't know what to say to follow it, which is why I was glad he ended up breaking the awkward silence.

"Hey," he said brightly. "There's a presentation by Gary Becker today in Lowell Hall. You wanna go?"

At the risk of sounding ignorant, I asked, "Who's that?"

"A famous economist known for the 'rotten kid theorem'. He's my favorite." Martin beamed. I loved how he got excited about economic topics and renowned economists during office hours. His energy was infectious—even making me excited about the stuff from time to time.

I wrinkled my brows. "What a great name for a theorem."

He chuckled. "Great name for a great theorem. Imagine a bad brother takes pleasure in harming his sister. If the parents say they'll give more inheritance money to the child who needs it more then the bad brother will want to help his sister do well so that he will end up getting more inheritance. His welfare has become dependent on the welfare of his sister. You can turn a bad boy into a good one with the proper incentives."

My brows scrunched further, pondering the example.

Martin shrugged then winked. "Maybe he's not famous enough."

I laughed. "It sounds interesting." And like a chance to hang out with a gorgeous guy. Besides, it wasn't often I got the chance to do leisurely things. "Sure, I'll go."

***

We began seeing more of each other. First neutral social events, then it became increasingly clear that we were dating. We'd been seeing each other for a few months when we walked by the gymnasium and Marty suggested we try out the swing dance club.

"A guy wanting to go dancing? I don't know, I'm not a very good dancer."

His full lips curved into a wicked grin. "Are you saying men can't dance?"

"Isn't that the stereotype?"

"Isn't it also the stereotype that girls are good at dancing?"

"Touché."

He put his arm out for me to grab and I took it gracefully. "Shall we?" he said.

I was surprised to find he wasn't only smart and handsome, but also a good dancer.

We spent the evening with our bodies close to one another, laughing and working up a sweat. I tripped over my feet and stepped on his multiple times but he didn't seem to mind. He helped show me how to do the basic moves and even convinced me to let him swing me around his waist.

It was the most fun I'd had in college to date.

***

"I've never done this before, Kristen. Have you?" His body was tense as he hovered over me on my bed in my dorm room. I had taken his shirt off and it was now lying on the floor where I'd thrown it. The surface of his sculpted torso was smooth and it was a major turn on to see it so up close. I'd been surprised to find he was amazingly fit for a nerdy teacher's assistant. A regular routine of swimming and dancing will do that to the body.

His chest was heaving as he tried to control his breathing.

I smiled. "If you're asking if I'm a virgin, I'd have to say no. I had a couple boyfriends in high school."

"I see." He averted his gaze from mine to look down at my chest, where he often liked to look. I didn't mind. In fact, I liked the way it made me feel desirable. He was usually so confident and in control but now in this intimate moment, he was vulnerable.

"Is that a problem?"

"No. . . I just never had a girlfriend before you. I'm kind of nervous."

I squinted my forehead.

"You look surprised."

"I am. I thought you'd have an extensive dating history given how smart and gorgeous you are."

He looked at me with those vivid blue eyes. "I don't trust others easily. I usually don't get too close to people."

"You trust me?" I gently pulled off his glasses and placed them on the bedside stand. His eyes became radiant.

"I trust you, Kristen."

"We'll go slow Marty. We'll take our time." I pulled one dress strap off my shoulder. I took his hand and placed it on my breast, releasing a slow breath as I felt the warmth radiating from his skin.

His cheeks flushed. It was so adorable to see him this way. "Kristen, I—I think I . . ."

"What is it?"

He shook his head. "Nothing. You're just so wonderful. The most amazing person I've ever met."

I smiled. "Even more amazing than Gary Becker?"

"A hundred times more amazing."

I tugged his brown hair and brought his lips down to mine. We made love that night for the first time.

***

Marty punched a fist-sized hole in the drywall of his apartment.

I was frightened. I'd seen small glimpses of his temper over the past few weeks—small outbursts over seemingly trivial things other people did—but I wasn't too concerned. I attributed it to stress. He was a TA and had a heavy course load after all. But his reactions had never gone this far.

"Marty, calm down. It's not a big deal."

"It is a big deal. How could he do that? Doesn't he have a conscience?"

"You're overreacting. He didn't mean it. He didn't see you coming so he accidentally opened the door and hit you in the face."

He sighed and rubbed his nose, which was beginning to swell up. He sat down on the brown suede couch next to me with his head in his hands.

"Why do you get so upset?" I asked. "Have you been stressed lately?" I began stroking his back gently. It was as much to soothe him as it was to soothe myself. I was still shaken up by that punch.

"No, I'm fine," he grumbled.

"Talk to me, Marty. You're not telling me something."

He didn't answer for a moment, preferring to rub his temples to calm himself. "I've never told anybody about this . . . sometimes I just get really angry. My mom was a bit harsh on me when I was growing up."

"What happened?"

He let out another long sigh. I could tell he was debating whether to say what was on his mind or not. "She was a drug addict." The words lingered in the air for a moment. "Even when she was pregnant with me, she was snorting cocaine. She says she's clean now but I know she still drinks a lot."

My heart ached for him. I knew what it was like to have a bad relationship with your parents. How it affected your social skills and your ability to relate to other people. You couldn't escape it no matter how far you ran. For me, moving from Texas to Massachusetts wasn't far enough. I thought I had it bad but it sounded like Marty had it even worse.

"I'm sorry to hear that," I said, continuing to rub his back to soothe him. "I didn't know."

He brightened unexpectedly. "Don't worry about it. It's in the past." He touched my cheek and kissed me. "I know I have a short fuse sometimes but I'm working on it. And you make me want to be better."

***

"Are you taking your medications?" I asked Marty. We were sitting in a secluded alcove of the Houghton library trying to study.

He had another bad episode recently when he punched a second hole in his wall because a professor criticized a point in one of his essays. The first hole had only been patched two months ago. We'd done it together with some do-it-yourself spackle from a nearby hardware store.

During that time, I'd recommended that he should see a therapist. He was reluctant at first but I finally convinced him to do it. After a few sessions, they told him he had borderline personality disorder, which meant his emotions were amplified and he was very impulsive. He could switch from extreme elation to extreme anger or depression quickly. All from a small trigger—slight criticism, a misunderstanding, etc.

His condition was both good and bad. The times he was happy, he was really happy, which made him the best person in the world to be around. He could brighten your day even if you had just attended a funeral that morning.

That was part of the reason girls—and even some men—were attracted to him like moths to a flame. He just had that kind of energy.

But the times he was unhappy, he was awful to be around. It was like a black cloud loomed over his head, tainting everything around him. He would rant and rave, exhibit bitterness, paranoia, and sometimes become physically violent—but he had never hurt me. I had a hard time believing such a wonderful person could become so terrible so quickly. It made me nervous that he could switch between the two extremes in a heartbeat.

Dr. Perkins had prescribed him medication that he was to take regularly. It was supposed to regulate his mood fluctuations. Make him more balanced like the average person. Less volatile.

"No. I can't think straight when I'm on them. I have to write this paper that's due tomorrow."

I felt extremely frustrated. "Do you care about me Marty?"

"Kristen, I care about you more than anything else. You know that."

"Yeah, Marty. I know. But you understand how it affects me when you don't take your meds right? It makes me scared." Tears began welling in my eyes. I didn't want to cry, but it was so frustrating not being able to get through to him. He needed help and I felt helpless in aiding him.

"Shh, shh." He put his arms around my shoulders and rubbed my arm up and down. "I'm sorry, Kristen. I'll take them."

I wiped tears from my face with my hand. "Are you going to your sessions?"

"Yeah I am . . . just not in the past few weeks."

"You need to go to your sessions," I said, trying my best not to sound like I was nagging.

"I know, but Dr. Perkins is a dolt. She doesn't understand me. I'm not getting much from talking with her."

"She's supposed to be one of the best therapists on the east coast for treating your condition. Please, Marty. Won't you do it for me?"

He took a deep breath then relaxed his shoulders. "Okay. I'll do it for you."

***

I'd just gotten back to my dorm room from a party to find Marty sitting on my bed waiting for me, his mouth a thin line. His apartment was further away from campus than my room so we'd been spending a lot of time at my place. It made sense for him to carry my extra key.

The first words out of his mouth were an accusation. "You don't care about me Kristen."

I didn't take to that greeting well. "I do, Marty. Damn it. I do."

"Then why did you go to that party when you knew it would only make me jealous?"

"God. I just went with some girls. They were nice enough to invite me. It's not like I have a lot of other friends here. I invited you but you said you had too much work to do."

"I know. I just hate the thought of other guys making a move on you. You're so beautiful. It drives me nuts to think you'd leave me for someone better. Someone more handsome and charming."

"I'd never cheat on you Marty. You have to trust me."

He grumbled then softened his voice. "I do trust you."

***

It was spring break and I didn't really want to go home to see my parents so I went to Marty's instead. He'd said they had a large house and his parents would be excited to meet me. His dad, Charles Pritchard, was a founding partner at one of the most prestigious law firms on the east coast so his family was financially very well off. It'd been a week since I arrived at the Pritchard household located on the outskirts of Boston and things weren't quite what I expected.

I was standing next to Marty in the living room. We were planning to go out for a dinner date but the car was gone and the other two cars were in the shop.

"Where's Dad?" Marty asked..

"He's out late again," Mrs. Pritchard said. She was sitting in a recliner aimed at the big screen TV but the TV wasn't on. She had a half-empty bottle of amber liquid in her hand. Even in her disheveled state, Melody Pritchard was a knockout for her age. Radiant blonde hair, hourglass body, and the face of a Victoria's Secret model. I could see how Marty got his good looks. She lived up to the "trophy" part of trophy wife for sure. "Probably at work banging the secretary." She brought the bottle to her lips for a long sip. "Nobody loves me. Not your father. Not you. My own son doesn't love his mother."

"I do, Mom. You know I do."

"I raised you. I gave you my tits to drink from. You made them saggy and ugly. That's why your father is cheating on me. Because I'm no longer pretty enough for him. How can I blame him for wanting other women?"

"No, Mom. Dad's just busy with work. He's not cheating."

She took another drink. "Men are all the same. Liars and cheaters. Isn't that right Kristen?"

This was awkward. Super awkward. *What was I supposed to say to that?*

". . . I don't know Mrs. Pritchard. Marty hasn't cheated on me. At least not that I know of. . ." I looked at Marty warily. He gave me a sympathetic look as if to say "I'm sorry you have to deal with this."

Mrs. Pritchard huffed then took another sip and gestured the bottle at me. "I like you. You're a good girl. I'm glad Marty met you." She turned her attention to Marty. "You be good to Kristen. She's such a nice girl. A real sweetheart. Don't you cheat on her like your no good father cheats on me."

"I'd never do that, Mom. I'm good. Just like you raised me."

She nodded. "That's right. You're a good boy, Martin. My son."

Mr. Pritchard didn't get back with the car until midnight that night. We ended up ordering delivery pizza and watching mindless action movies in Marty's room. I faintly heard Mr. Pritchard and his wife arguing downstairs but most of it was drowned out by the explosions and gunshots blaring from the TV.

***

"What do you think about the idea of having kids someday?" Marty asked, his hands behind his head. I was leaning against his chest still coming off the buzz of a recent orgasm.

We'd just had angry make-up sex after having a heated argument over someone—a guy—leaving a benign comment on my Facebook wall. We fought, I ended up deleting it, then we humped like rabbits. It was becoming a more frequent occurrence.

I laughed and looked up at him. "Aren't we jumping the gun here a bit? I haven't even graduated yet."

He smiled. "Just a hypothetical question."

"I don't know. I haven't given it too much thought. Kids are cute when they're babies but even then they're a handful. I can't imagine how rough it'd be when they become teenagers. I'm not sure I'm fit to be a mother. Lord knows I haven't had a good reference."

"I think you'd make a great mom."

I laughed again. "That's quite a compliment. Care to provide some reasons to back up your claim Mr. Know-It-All?"

"You're very caring. Compassionate. You know what not to be like."

"Doesn't mean I know what *to* be like."

His smile widened and he winked one blue eye. "I have faith in you. You're a quick learner."

He was poking fun of me so I tickled his ribs because I knew he hated that. "How about you? What do you think of being a dad?"

"I'm looking forward to it someday, definitely. Settle down. Be a good father. I'd spend a lot of time with the kid and give a lot of attention, that's for sure."

"You're not going to be busy all the time like your dad?"

"I'd try my hardest not to be. I definitely don't want to be like that."

I began to think about what it would be like raising a kid with Marty. Just keeping our relationship on the tracks was hard enough because of his condition, I couldn't imagine what it would be like if we added a child to the mix.

"You're thinking about something," he said. "What is it?"

I shook my head. "Oh it's nothing."

"C'mon, you can tell me." He stroked my hair gently. "Don't worry, you're not going to upset me."

"Okay," I said softly. "I was going to ask if you were worried about your condition, if it'll be passed on to the baby."

He paused to think about it. "Supposedly, part of it is genetic so it's possible it could be passed down. But it's definitely not certain." After a moment he smiled. "If it happens, you can be there to keep us both in line."

***

"Why would you drop out of law school?" I asked.

We were in my apartment in Boston. I'd already graduated and been working at a financial company for a few months. Marty was going to Yale Law School in Connecticut but had shown up at my place unexpectedly. We'd been on and off for close to a year now. Things started getting rockier after he went to law school. Every time I'd break up with him, he'd apologize profusely and promise to change. I'd forgive him and we'd try again. It was complicated between us.

This was one of our off cycles.

He shrugged. "It was pointless. I hated it."

"But you were going to work at your dad's firm right? What's he going to say?"

"He can go screw himself," Marty huffed. "That's all he cares about: his law firm. He'll probably be pissed and cut me off financially but whatever. I'm sure I'll find something else to do."

"Marty, it doesn't sound like you've thought this through. You're over halfway done. Why not just finish it?"

"It's stupid. I never wanted to do it anyway. My dad just forced me to do it. Having his son go to the top law school in the country makes him look good. He doesn't really care about me."

"You're upset, Marty. Let's think about this."

"No one cares about me. Dad's never around. Mom's a mess. You're all I have Kristen."

I inhaled air into my lungs to compose myself. "We can't keep doing this, Marty. It's getting tiring. We go through the same thing over and over again."

"I'm tired too but we love each other too much." He stared into my eyes. The intense gaze from those blue irises bore through layers of doubt and uncertainty. "We both know we'll never be over."

***

I shoved clothes and items into my luggage in a hurry. My pinky still hurt, which made it difficult picking things up with my right hand. I needed to get out of here. Get out of Boston.

Thankfully I didn't have much stuff. The apartment had been fully furnished when I moved in. All my essential things fit into two large suitcases—at least they did after I smooshed everything together. Everything else I could leave behind.

As for the email and Facebook passwords, I'd have to change them when I got to New York.

I needed to start over.

Chapter Two

The pounding at my apartment door became a quiet knock after I told him to go away. The controlled response irritated me. How could Vincent act so cool after I'd just found out he cheated on me with Ariel? *That asshole had some nerve showing up at my doorstep.* I was going to open the door and scream at him. He was a wolf in sheep's clothing and he'd fooled me.

The worst part though—he wasn't the first.

I twisted back the deadbolt, but purposefully left the chain lock in place. Vincent wasn't coming inside—not unless he begged. And even then, probably not. I opened the door a crack and glanced at the man standing on my welcome mat.

I froze.

It wasn't Vincent at the other side of the door.

Piercing blue eyes. Square, rimless glasses. Tousled brown hair parted down the center.

It was Marty.

My hand instinctively leaped to the heart-shaped necklace around my neck. *How could this be happening?* I'd been so consumed with Vincent and work lately that I nearly forgot he had shown up at my apartment a month ago when only Riley was home.

"Kristen! I'm so glad I found you. I've been so worried." The familiar crisp, masculine voice flowed over me, halting my breath. He placed one hand over his heart while keeping the other one behind his back. He was wearing a black v-neck over jeans that led down to brown suede boots. The casual, laid-back appearance contrasted sharply with my reaction to seeing this man on my doorstep.

"Marty?" I wanted to shut the door, to run away, to change addresses again. Maybe change my name this time. But I couldn't move. My hands and feet had turned to ice.

"Wow, you look amazing." He smiled as his eyes scanned up and down my body. "Even better than I remember. I don't know how that's possible."

I became acutely aware that I was still wearing the hip-hugging black dress I'd worn to dinner with Vincent. My hair was still styled but my makeup was a mess after crying over Vincent's infidelity.

"H-How did you find me?"

"When I went to your place in Boston, I found out you weren't there. I didn't know where you went until I typed your name into Google recently and found this address."

That's insanely strange. I regularly Googled myself to make sure my new address never showed up on the internet for that very reason. I knew my company never posted specific employee information on their website. Had I slipped up somehow?

He continued. "I want to say I'm so so sorry for everything I've put you through. I know why you left in such a hurry and I can't blame you."

Tears caught in my throat as I recalled the traumatic moments of my pinky being twisted. A flood of conflicting emotions confused me. Fear. Relief. Pain. Hope. Good and bad memories flashed through my mind. Office hours. Swing dancing. Nights we made love. Days we screamed at each other. His fist going into the wall. We'd been together for two and a half years and I thought I'd locked away those memories in some dark recess of my brain but all of it came crashing down on me now like an avalanche.

"I know I can't ever take things back. I should've called but I knew I had to tell you this in person."

My grip on the necklace tightened. He was right. He shouldn't have just shown up on my doorstep unannounced. Not the first time. Not like this. I glanced warily at his other hand, which was still behind his back. I clicked off the safety on my mace necklace preparing for what he might do after what I was about to say to him.

"Marty, you shouldn't be here."

His blue eyes shifted. A subtle cover slid over them that changed their appearance to pleading. "I'm sorry. I'm so so sorry. I've been working on myself. I've been seeing Dr. Perkins. I haven't given up on us."

"That was two years ago," I stuttered. "I've moved on. I needed to start over."

A flinch in his features betrayed frustration. For a brief instant his eyes flickered intensity. It was the same look as when he punched a hole in his apartment wall. But as soon as it appeared, it disappeared. "Don't give up on me, Kristen. We've been through so much together. We've shared things we've never shared with anyone else. Don't throw that all away."

"You threw it all away. After what you did to me . . ." My hands trembled and my legs felt weak. I staggered against the wall for support. My body burned and my skin prickled. I could feel my heart beating rapidly. I wanted to shout, cry, push, shove, and throw my hands up in defeat all at the same. It was a strangely familiar feeling. Like I had sunk back into an old routine I'd learned to break.

And then I realized: after two years, we were arguing again.

"It was out of line, I know. I won't do it again, I promise. I've been working on myself these years we've been apart." He smiled in frustration. "You've got to listen to me."

How many times had he made promises before? He'd always broken them. He wouldn't take his meds. He wouldn't see his therapist. I'd wanted to believe in him time and time again. A part of me even wanted to believe him now. That he'd finally changed for better. But instinct won out. "No, Marty. No."

"Please, Kristen," he said softly. He pulled his hand out from behind his back. Surprised, I took a step back. In his hand was a bouquet of blue flowers. "I brought you these. Bluebonnets, your favorite."

I was shocked. He'd remembered an offhand comment I'd made when we had visited the botanical gardens while we were still dating. He'd asked me which flower was my favorite and I'd said the bluebonnet because it reminded me of Texas and the color matched his stunning blue eyes.

My heart stopped in my chest. The anger, frustration, fear—all of it disappeared for a moment.

He stepped forward and extended his open palm through the narrow opening of the door. I could've shut the door before, but now if I tried it would mean shutting it on his hand.

"I'll never hurt you again," he said softly.

"Marty, I—"

His fingers nearly touching my hand at my necklace, I became painfully aware of my pinky throbbing. I didn't know what to do. It was happening all over again. The helplessness. The frustration. The desire to please. The hope that things would be different this time. The fear that they wouldn't be.

Then his fingers touched my hand. The next moment happened too quick for me to process. When my brain caught up, I saw Marty toppling across the floor. A short but muscular body in a striped polo had tackled him to the ground scattering blue flowers across the hallway.

"Bernie!" I screamed, recognizing his orange tan.

Where did he come from? What the hell was he doing? What was going on?

"Get off me!" Marty cried as he struggled to free himself from Bernie's bearhug from behind.

The two men rolled across the dusty hallway carpet, wrestling for dominance, kicking the ground, kicking the wall, crushing flowers in their wake. Bernie slid his bearhug high and managed to wrap his arm around Marty's neck for a chokehold. Marty grasped at Bernie's arm trying to pry it away but the arm was too strong and muscular; within moments, Marty's face became red from lack of circulation.

Growling and gritting his teeth, Marty pushed himself off the floor with Bernie still on his back hovering a foot off the ground. Marty threw his back against the wall, slamming Bernie so hard it felt like the whole apartment building shook. It was enough to loosen Bernie's grip and

Marty took advantage of the opportunity. He adjusted his chin and bit down on Bernie's forearm causing Bernie to release the hold. Marty staggered away but not before kicking Bernie in the face, making him reel backward.

"You fucking moron, messing with me," Marty cried, gasping for air. He faltered on his feet fighting against dizziness to regain his balance while Bernie leaned against the wall recovering from the damage he'd taken, spitting out blue petals from his mouth—and a tooth—in the process.

A tall man with long, toned arms swiftly moved behind Marty like a ninja and grabbed one of his arms and pulled it behind his back while twisting his wrist. It was professional, like something a police officer would do. How did Kurt know how to do that?

I unlatched the chain on the door and rushed into the hallway—not caring about how I looked.

"Stand back, Kristen." Kurt yelled. "We're not going to let him hurt you. We're here to protect you." Kurt pushed

Marty down onto the ground and Bernie jumped on top of Marty's back to hold him still with his weight.

"W-what?" I stammered. I had no idea what was going on. It was all happening too fast.

"Kristen, I wasn't going to hurt you!" Marty shouted from his face-down position pinned beneath Bernie.

"He wasn't going to do anything," I cried.

"It's our job—" Kurt tightened Marty's arm behind his back, making him yelp. "To protect you."

I shook my head in disbelief, frantically trying to grasp the situation. "I don't understand."

"Please. Get back inside the apartment Ms. Daley," said Bernie whose nose and mouth were bleeding from Marty's kick.

"Why? How did you know my last name?"

I was about to ask more questions when I heard footsteps bounding up the stairwell. Had somebody in one of the other apartments heard the commotion and reported it? Was it the police?

An imposing figure in elegant dress clothes appeared at the top of the stairs. His breathing was fast and his dark eyes were fierce.

Vincent. He looked as if he had come straight from the restaurant where I left him.

Noticing me along with the commotion nearby, a grave look swept over his features. He dashed down the hallway toward us, his black loafers thumping like hooves against the dingy carpet.

"Vincent!" I cried. I was surprised by the relief I felt at seeing him.

Vincent stopped in front of us, his face marred with concern. He gently gripped my shoulders. "Kristen, are you all right? Are you hurt in any way?" His usual composure in dangerous situations was gone.

"I-I'm fine, Vincent. But it's crazy. There's a fight . . . I don't know what to do. I'm scared." Everything was happening so fast, I couldn't form the proper words to explain. Even if I could, he wouldn't believe me. How could I explain that Marty had shown up unexpectedly with flowers and then my seriously muscular neighbor who likes Lady Gaga tackled him thinking he was going to hurt me? Even I'd have trouble believing me.

I was glad Vincent was here now though. Once again, I became aware of how Vincent made me feel safe. He'd put an end to this drama.

Vincent turned his gaze to Marty being held on the ground. Marty was still struggling, cursing. Vincent's jaw became tight and his eyes a blazing inferno. "You think you can use fear to control her? I'll show you fear." Vincent clenched his hands. "Bring him to his knees," he said.

Kurt and Bernie brought Marty up to his knees while continuing to restrain him. Marty tried to resist but Kurt tightened the hold on his arm. As Vincent stood in front of Marty kneeling, I could tell that they had similar heights and builds. They glared at each other fiercely like two wild lions ready to fight over a female. The similarity between them was jarring.

"What are you doing Vincent?" I cried. Vincent ignored me. His focus was solely on Marty.

"You son of a bitch." Vincent pulled his arm back and swung, landing a clean blow across Marty's cheek. Marty's glasses flew off his head and slammed against the nearby wall. I thought I heard somebody's bone crack. I wasn't sure if it was Marty's jaw or Vincent's knuckle.

"What are you doing?" I screamed.

"Why'd you hit me you piece of shit? I'll fucking kill you," Marty yelled.

"You think you're tough beating up women?" Vincent snarled.

He took another swing with his other hand, landing a blow on Marty's other cheek.

"You just want to control her. You have no right."

"Fuck you. You don't know shit about me!" Marty cried.

Then Vincent began kicking him in the stomach.

"Go to hell," Marty panted in between blows.

"You don't care about her. You never did."

I'd never seen this side of Vincent before. He punched Marty again and again as if possessed. I watched in horror as a realization swept over me: Marty was going to die.

I leaped in front of Vincent to shield Marty. Vincent pulled his punch back as I wrapped my arms around him and buried my face into his chest.

"Stop Vincent! Please, god. Stop. You're going to kill him!"

His body tensed. His arm raised up to strike. I closed my eyes and prepared myself for the worst. Then suddenly I felt his body relax. Vincent's arm slowly came down to his side.

"You come anywhere near Kristen again and I'll fucking kill you."

"You want us to take him away, boss?" Kurt asked.

Boss? Why did Kurt just call him boss? How did he know Vincent?

"Wait." Vincent gently gripped my waist and moved me to the side. He stepped toward Marty and grabbed him by the hair lifting his head to stare into his eyes. "Tell me you understand."

Marty gurgled something incomprehensible, his eyes half-dazed.

"Nod your head if you understand."

Vincent released his grip on Marty's head and Marty nodded faintly.

"Take care of him," Vincent said to Kurt.

Kurt nodded and stooped to pick up Marty's glasses. He and Bernie dragged Marty off by the arms toward the stairwell. Marty put up no resistance this time, his feet dragging along ground.

I couldn't believe what Vincent just said. Were they going to murder Marty in cold blood? Frantically, I asked, "You're not going to kill him are you?"

Vincent looked at me intensely; his brows narrowed into sharp lines frightened me. "Of course not. That was never going to happen. They'll patch him up and send him away, and then I'll have them keep an eye on him to make sure he never comes back. Kurt and Bernie are pros. You're safe now."

"You almost killed him! What the fuck is wrong with you?" I began to pound on his chest with my hands, tears forming in my eyes.

He gripped my arms firmly and stared deep into my eyes. The blazing inferno from earlier was gone, replaced by an equally fierce tenderness. "I needed to make sure he wasn't going to hurt you again."

"But—"

"Look, let's go inside before the neighbors call the police. I'll explain everything."

I was still shaking when Vincent put his arm around my shoulders. He ushered me inside, stepping on blue petals in the process.

I entered my apartment with Vincent's warm arm around my shoulder. My eyes stung with tears. Thoughts raced through my mind in a swirl. I was flooded with questions.

He gestured to the couch to have a seat but I turned to him as soon as he closed the door behind us. "What the fuck was that Vincent?" I spat. "Why were my neighbors going badass commando on Marty?"

His calm facade had returned and he reached out to wipe the tears from my cheek. "They were the security team I hired to keep an eye on you."

My world spun. I could feel the blood draining from my face. I no longer knew what was real and what wasn't. "You hired a security team?"

"Yes, to watch over you. To keep you safe."

The neutral tone of his response infuriated me. "What the hell? I thought you were half-joking about that."

His expression became unexpectedly dark. "I'd never joke about something like that."

"We talked about this. I told you I didn't want one and you agreed to that. That's why we went to Grandpa Rambo's store on the outskirts of town for mace. You didn't listen to me. You lied to me."

He grimaced. "I did it because I care about you Kristen. It was for your own protection."

"My protection? God. What's wrong with you? This isn't the wild west, Vincent. Seriously, you almost killed a man today."

His mouth was a thin line. "Maybe he deserved it."

"Jesus, I feel like I don't even know you. One minute you're nice and charming, the next you're a violent psychopath. You and your security team beat up a single man like some kind of goon squad. I was expecting the couple across the hall to maybe ask for a cup of sugar every now and then, not turn out to be fucking mercenaries."

His features twisted in pain. "Please, Kristen. I'm sorry. I did lie to you but please understand I had to ensure your safety."

"Keeping me safe is one thing. wailing on Marty like some kind of mobster is another. That crossed a ton of lines. Why didn't you break his legs with a baseball bat while you were at it? Or better yet, cut off one of his fingers. How do I know that's not what's happening right now?"

"I know it seems extreme but believe me, it was necessary. I've seen guys like him before. I know they don't give up easily. I wouldn't have gone that far if I didn't think it was necessary."

I put my hands on my hips. "You've seen guys like him before? Where? Some TV show?"

Vincent sighed deeply. "My sister Giselle had an abusive boyfriend. That's how I know."

I grunted in frustration. He was dropping bomb after bomb on me, destroying pieces of reality I thought I had a hold on. "Okay. Why didn't you tell me about this?"

"I didn't feel comfortable talking about it. And I didn't know if I could trust you before."

"Trust me?" I threw my hands up. "I told you secrets about myself I hadn't told anyone and you were holding back on me. What better time were you going to get to tell me than that night in your apartment when I spilled to you about Marty? But no, you didn't trust me, even after I took such a risk by trusting you, Vincent. How is that supposed to make me feel?"

"I was focused on your problem, Kristen. I wanted to keep it about you."

"Showing me you understood would have been about me, Vincent. Holding out on me while you made plans about my privacy is about you."

"You're right, Kristen. It was selfish. I'm sorry I didn't see it that way before. I was trying to do what I thought was best. Hopefully you see that, even if you disagree with my actions." He gently rested his hand on my shoulder.

Despite enjoying the sensation, I shrugged it off. "I don't trust you now though. You lied to me. You fucked Ariel Diamond. You cheated on me. At least Marty never did that." I tried shoving him away but he was like a wall. Instead it was me that fell backward. He grabbed me before I could fall on my ass.

"Hang on, Kristen. Listen to me," he growled, raising the hairs on the back of my neck. "That is all a mistake. The text you saw from Ariel wasn't what it looked like."

"How gullible do you think I am? What else could it mean? It was pretty clear: she liked riding your cock," I spat. The words tasted like battery acid coming off my tongue. I regained my footing and pushed out of his arms. He stepped forward and pulled my waist to him demonstrating his persistence. I knew I wouldn't win a battle of wills with him so I let it pass.

"She meant my surfboard. The new product my company launched—which is why I went to Brazil. It's called the *Shuttlecock*." He articulated his words carefully but assertively.

What. The. Fuck.

The room spun. "You're lying," I said uncertainly.

"No." His voice softened and his eyes carried the tenderness they had earlier. "I'm not lying. I'm sorry you saw that, but Ariel was just being flippant in that text like she usually is. It's her personality. You saw how she was when you met her. I'm sure she had no idea you'd be seeing that message. Even she's not that much of a trouble-maker."

A wave of embarrassment washed over me. I'd run out of the restaurant upset over a misunderstanding. Realization that my actions must've seemed absolutely childish to him made me pissed off. At him.

"'Shuttlecock?' You have to be kidding me. That's the stupidest name I've ever heard."

He allowed himself a smile. "You thought 'Pier Pleasure' was pretty clever."

"That at least makes sense. Shuttlecock makes no sense."

He took a deep breath and sighed. "You're right, it's dumb. But it's edgy and it's selling well. As you can see, people love making cock jokes."

I took a step back and folded my arms across my chest. I eyed him sternly. "So you didn't have sex with Ariel?"

"No. God no. I haven't even seen her since the time we ran into her on St. Lucia. I told you we're just friends and have been for years. I'd never cheat on you Kristen. Now *that* would be stupid. Unbelievably stupid."

My arms tightened. "I don't know if I can believe you."

"It's true. There's not much I can do to prove it so you're just going to have to trust me."

"I've trusted you all this time. But now with the whole security team thing, you going psycho, Giselle, and everything else, I don't know what to think. What else are you hiding from me?"

"Ask me anything. I'll tell you."

I clenched my jaw. "But I don't even know what to ask, Vincent. You can't do that—put the blame on me for not asking the right questions."

"No, Kitten. That's not how I meant it."

After lying to me, he was still calling me Kitten? Give me a break. "Don't call me that. You've lost that privilege."

He exhaled heavily and gestured to the living room. "Okay, let's sit down on the couch, cool off, and talk."

Because my feet were getting tired, I begrudgingly obeyed. Once we were seated, I ran through in my mind what I had just learned, deciding what to ask. There were so many pieces missing that needed filling in. I decided to start with the first question on my mind. "So what happened with Giselle?"

He shifted in his seat beside me. "She was in a relationship with someone she met in college for two years. Jim. No one knew she was suffering. There were small signs like arguing but it seemed normal—couples usually have fights every now and then. It wasn't until I saw her bruises that . . . that I decided I needed to intervene. I made sure he got the message." He sighed.

"I'm sorry about what happened to your sister, but in this case you took it too far. Way too far. You didn't have to break Marty's face. He wasn't going to hurt me."

"What did he want?"

"He said he just wanted to talk."

Vincent's eyes narrowed as he ground his teeth. "I wouldn't believe him. That's a classic trick they use. He hurt you before. That's enough to establish that he's dangerous."

"He said he was sorry and brought me flowers. He just wanted to apologize."

"You don't know that Kristen. Kurt and Bernie were watching. If they made a move, it meant they thought you were in danger."

"You don't know either. He was just extending his hand to say sorry. Last time I checked that wasn't a felony."

He looked at me probingly. "Why are you defending him?"

"Jesus, Vincent. Can you be any more insensitive? I'm not defending him." My eyes began tearing again. "Don't treat me like I'm a helpless victim. I can't stand it."

"My team will make sure you won't be."

"Why aren't you listening to me?" I screamed. "Get rid of them! I hate the idea of being watched and monitored."

He kept his gaze firmly on me as I broke down. "Kristen, he might come back. You have to take this seriously."

"You nearly killed him for bringing me flowers, Vincent! I doubt he'd be coming back. I think he 'got the message'."

He quietly handed me a tissue. I took it and wiped my eyes, pulling mascara off in the process. I knew I looked like a mess but I didn't care.

"I don't like it. I want you to feel safe. If he does come back, you'll be completely exposed."

I closed my eyes for a moment and forced out a shaky breath. "Right now, I'm more afraid of you than I am of him."

He narrowed his brows. "You don't mean that."

I looked at him directly. "I do. You don't know what it's like watching your boyfriend nearly beat your ex to death. I'm scared of you and what you're capable of."

Vincent staggered back for a moment, no doubt reeling from my response. "All right, fine. I'll get rid of the security team. I'll tell them to put a tracking device on his car so we can monitor his whereabouts." He stared into my eyes. "But you should know that I'd never hurt you."

"You already have. Maybe not physically like Marty did, but you hurt me emotionally. You betrayed my trust."

"Okay. How can I make this right?"

I shook my head. "I don't know if you can."

"I really care about you Kristen and if you need space, I can do that." He got up from the couch. "But if I had to choose between us breaking up and you being safe, without a doubt I'd choose the latter. I wouldn't be able to live with myself if you got hurt and I had the ability to prevent it. I'd even lie to you if it meant saving you from harm."

"You can't do that. You can't take away my choice from me. I'm a grown woman who can make her own choices balancing her privacy and her safety. You made it your choice."

"It's what happens when you—" He cut his sentence short. "When you really care about someone. If you're asking if I'd do it again. I'll tell you right now: I'd do it in a heartbeat."

After he left, I locked the door. Then I went to my room to cry.

***

I'd cried until I felt nauseous from everything and vomited. It was incredible the police didn't show up. The commotion from the fighting, shouting, and cursing was probably heard on multiple floors. I didn't know my other neighbors on the floor that well but I knew they were in their mid-twenties. They were probably out clubbing. It was Friday night after all.

I walked from the bathroom to the kitchen to get a cup of water. It was past midnight and I was exhausted from the evening's events. I couldn't wait to fall asleep and block everything out until tomorrow. During a long sip of water, the front door unlocked, opened, and clacked against the chain lock.

"Kristen? You left the chain lock on. Open up."

I nearly choked on my water before I recognized the voice.

"Riley, is that you? Are you by yourself?"

"Uh yeah, duh. Were you expecting someone else?" She jiggled the door again but it wouldn't budge. "Are you naked right now with whip cream on your nipples waiting for Vincent to show up? Is that why there are flower petals all over the doormat?"

I breathed a sigh of relief. Typical Riley. "No, I'm not naked," I hollered. "I'll open the door." I went to undo the chain. Once she was inside, I redid the chain.

The short blue dress she went out in was rumpled and there were drink stains on it. She must've danced pretty hard, even if she'd gotten in early. "So how was dinner?" she asked.

I groaned. "Bad."

"Bad? Or badass?" Riley said, her mood chipper as she flung off her shoes into the corner.

When I didn't respond, she looked at me and studied my face. "Whoa Kristen, were you crying? Oh my god, what happened?"

I told her about how I saw Ariel's text message during dinner with Vincent and how I ran home and then Marty showed up.

Riley dropped her bags, gripped my shoulders, and shook me. "Are you okay? Did you call the police?"

"No. Kurt and Bernie tackled him. Turns out they were Vincent's security team he assigned to watch over me."

She squinted. "You mean the gay couple across from us?"

I wasn't sure about the gay couple part. In fact, I didn't know what to believe about Kurt and Bernie. They could've been Navy SEALs or trained killers for all I knew. "Yeah."

"No way." She put her hand up to my forehead to check my temperature.

"Yes way. They restrained Marty and Vincent showed up and beat the shit out of him. I thought Vincent was going to kill him."

Riley gasped. "Wow! I'm sure he was just protecting you though, right?"

"Yeah, but it was way overboard. Marty wasn't even doing anything threatening. We were just talking outside my door when he was tackled."

Her voice lowered. "But he could have done something. It can happen in a split second."

I shook my head. "Still. You don't go as far as Vincent did. He was punching and kicking Marty so hard I thought he was going to die. Plus, he lied to me. He asked me before if I wanted a security team and I told him no and he ignored my answer completely. It makes me feel so small and powerless!" I began to cry.

Riley pulled me to her and hugged me. "It's okay. You're safe now."

I sobbed into her shoulder. "I don't know what to do, Riley."

"Are you afraid Vincent's going to hurt you?" Her words were careful.

"No, I don't think he'll hurt me. But then again I didn't know he was capable of what he did to Marty. I don't know if I can trust him. I don't know what to think."

"You said he cheated on you with that chick Ariel, right? Then fuck him. Let him go surfing with sharks and have his dick get bitten off."

"I saw a text from Ariel saying she enjoyed riding his cock—and I freaked out. But Vincent explained that she was referring to his company's new surfboard called the Shuttlecock."

She pulled back and looked at me. "Are you serious? You have to be kidding." She laughed. "That's hilarious. What a clever name."

"No it's not! It's stupid."

"A shuttlecock in badminton moves back and forth through the air—kind of like how a surfboard moves across a wave. Plus it has the word 'cock' in it. You have to admit that's pretty genius marketing."

Apparently I wasn't the target audience. "You're the worst."

She laughed. "Aw, I'm sorry Kris. I'm listening." She led me by the hand and we took a seat on the couch.

Riley whipped out her phone and began pecking at it. "Looks like there really is a surfboard named that. It's got rave reviews already. People are saying they love the handling but the best part is the name. So I don't think he was lying to you. It was just an innocent misunderstanding."

"He lied about the security team though. And he acted like a psycho. He told me it was because his younger sister Giselle had an abusive boyfriend and he beat that guy up."

"Sounds like he's a knight with shining abs."

Her tone was starting to piss me off. I needed my best friend to take me seriously. "Or a guy with a temper problem. I never knew Vincent had that side to him."

That wiped the smile off her face. "Stop it. Vincent's totally different from Marty. He had a good reason for doing what he did. Marty hurt you before and I can see why Vincent reacted the way he did. Hell, if I was here when Marty showed up, I'd probably mace first, ask questions later."

She put her phone back in her pocket and rested her hand on my knee. "Give Vincent a chance. He's not perfect. You showed him your baggage, now he's shown you his. Take some time to think about it."

That was a good point about baggage. "I get where Vincent's coming from, but I don't know if we're going to work out. There's so much drama in my life—Vincent, Marty, work stuff. I really wish things were simpler. I don't know if I can handle all the chaos right now. I'm pretty close to a total breakdown."

Riley looked at me searchingly. "Are you thinking of breaking up with Vincent?"

I sighed. "Maybe. Or at least taking a break from our relationship."

She took my hand gently in hers. "To me it sounds like Vincent really cares about you. And I mean really. He got you a freaking security team. And from what you've told me over the past few weeks, you really care about him too. Am I right?"

"Of course I care about him."

"This is only your first fight as a couple, right?"

"Well, it's our second. The first one happened after I met Ariel. This one is much bigger."

"So it's your first major fight. That's pretty normal considering how long you've been seeing each other. I usually have major fights in the first few weeks."

"The circumstances aren't normal at all. Lying about security teams and mauling exes isn't normal."

"Lies are pretty common, Kris. People have been forgiven for far worse lies than covering up an attempt to be overprotective against a psycho ex-boyfriend."

I rolled my eyes. "That's a strong case."

Her blue eyes became serious. "Kristen, you've always been afraid of consequences since I've known you. You're afraid of getting hurt and that makes perfect sense given what you've been through. Your relationship with Vincent is a risk for sure. He could hurt you emotionally but you could also hurt him. But what relationship isn't a risk? Sometimes you have to take a risk because the reward is worth it."

I groaned. "You sound like Vincent talking about risk-taking."

She smiled. "Do I? Have you considered that maybe Vincent sounds like me?"

A grin spread on my lips. I didn't know how she did it, but Riley always knew how to make me smile in the worst circumstances. "He definitely does not sound like you. You've got a dirtier mind."

Her smile turned wicked. "And proud of it. So are you going to be okay? Or do we need to go to Savage Hunks to cheer you up? They're still open at this hour you know."

The last thing I needed right now was to see more muscled men causing a commotion. I needed peace tonight. "As tempting as that sounds, I think I'm okay now. At least a lot better than before."

She squeezed my hand. "I'll be here for you, whatever you need."

I squeezed her hand back. "Thanks Riley."

***

I didn't have work the next day since it was Saturday. Thank goodness because I didn't think I'd be able to get any work done with everything spinning in my mind. Although I had been exhausted the previous night, I still had difficulty falling asleep.

Unfortunately, that didn't stop me from waking up at the usual seven. Habit can be a bitch sometimes.

I immediately checked my phone and realized I had turned it off the previous night. Remembering why I had done so, I chose to leave it off. Still groggy but unusually hungry, I decided to start the morning with a big breakfast of eggs, bacon, and sausage, hoping the meal would help me fall back asleep.

Fortunately it did the trick. I ended up sleeping well into the afternoon. I woke up and immediately went to the couch to veg out in front of the TV. There was a lot on my mind and I wanted to drown it out, which is why I tuned into Bridezillas—my guilty pleasure. Except I felt no guilt watching it, only pure unadulterated pleasure.

Just when a bride's grandmother said she looked like a slut in her chosen wedding gown, I heard a rustling across the hall. I looked out my peephole and saw Kurt and Bernie moving boxes from their apartment. I'd barely gotten to know them and they were already moving out. Bernie's face was looking a lot better without all the blood, although it was a bit swollen. His deep tan made it less noticeable, though.

I thought about stepping out to say something to them but everything I could think of sounded awkward: "Thanks for beating up my ex-boyfriend yesterday . . . I think? How do you two know Vincent? So . . . do you guys tan together?"

I ended up watching them for a few minutes then returning to my show.

They didn't have much stuff, so after a few hours, I heard them finish and lock up. I spent the rest of the day vegging out on the couch, thinking about my situation.

I was still upset with Vincent even though I knew he cared about me and I cared about him. It only made it that much more painful that he lied to me. There were trust issues Vincent and I had to work out and that would take time and effort.

Then there was the issue of work. Carl was feeding me opportunities and I'd been snapping them up, which made me busier and busier. Vincent seemed to be in a similar situation with his company occupying most of his time the past few weeks.

Even though my employers hadn't found out about my relationship with Vincent, it was still becoming a problem. It needed work and neither of us had the time to do it—at least not without making significant sacrifices.

When the latest episode ended with the bride literally pulling chunks of her own hair out, I came to the conclusion that I was going to take a break from my relationship with Vincent. I couldn't keep going with things the way they were. If I didn't make a change, I would lose my mind.

**

On Sunday afternoon I finally gave in to turning on my phone. I was going to call Vincent and tell him we should take a break. Closing my bedroom door, I picked up my phone from the nightstand and turned it on. There were a bunch of unread text messages—some of them new and some of them from Friday when I ran out of the restaurant.

I ignored the messages and called him.

He answered on the first ring. "Kristen?"

His silky voice had its usual effect on me even though I knew to prepare for it. "Vincent . . ."

He released an audible exhale and I could picture his chest lowering from the release of air. "I'm so glad to hear your voice. I thought I wasn't going to hear from you again and that scared me."

"Hey Vincent. Listen . . . I need to tell you something." I had to push this conversation forward before Vincent's persuasive hold took effect. Otherwise, I'd begin doubting my decision. Fortunately, it was much easier to resist him on the phone than in person.

"Wait. Just a moment." I heard some mumbling in the background. "Shit. I'm sorry, Kristen. I have a meeting right now. But whatever you want to tell me sounds important. Is it an emergency? Can I meet you later? I'll try my hardest to be done by six."

"You're at work on a Sunday?"

There was another mumble in the background. "Yeah, sorry. We have a lot going on over here right now."

I breathed deeply, reaffirmed in my decision that we were both too busy to make this work. "I'll drop by your office at six thirty then."

Meeting him at his office as opposed to his place or my place would make it easier to leave after the discussion. It would've been easier just to tell him over the phone but I supposed it was more appropriate to handle this in person.

His voice brightened. "Can't wait to see you then."

"Bye Vincent."

When evening rolled around, I gingerly stepped out my front door in jeans and a t-shirt. It'd been nearly two days since I left the apartment. I made sure to pack my taser in my purse before I went over to Vincent's office in case I ran into any more trouble along the way.

As expected, the commute downtown was less crowded than usual since most people weren't working. High-powered CEOs were one of the exceptions. I made it to the Red Fusion offices to find a few people crunching on their laptops. I was about to ring Vincent when an employee who recognized me from before kindly opened the glass door. I thanked him and he promptly returned to his desk to work on his keyboard. Knowing the way to Vincent's office, I walked down the hall and stopped in front of his door. This wasn't going to be an easy discussion, but it had to be done.

I took a deep breath then went inside.

Vincent was at his desk, brows furrowed and typing furiously. He was in his usual elegant New York attire: white shirt with red-striped tie and black pants. When he saw me—those dark brown eyes piercing me like arrows—he stopped working and smiled. "Kristen."

"Hey," I said, returning his smile. I kept one hand in my jeans and waved at him with the other.

He glided around the desk and hugged me tightly, the squeeze making my legs turn to jelly momentarily. As always, he smelled wonderful. The spicy scent tickled my nostrils as well as other parts of my body. He kissed me on the forehead then the tip of my nose. "I'm so glad you're here. I thought you'd call so I could let you in."

"I was going to when one of your employees let me inside," I said as he led me by the hand to his leather couch in the corner. I was reminded of the first time I entered this office intending to make another case for choosing Waterbridge-Howser as his wealth management firm but wound up almost having sex with him instead. That was a distressing time in my life but not quite as distressing as recent events.

"I got you these." He reached for the coffee table and handed me a bouquet of red roses. There was a card attached with a small puffin on the front. It looked rough, like it was drawn with crayons by a child.

"Did you draw this picture?" I asked.

"Yeah, you like it?" He sounded proud of his work.

I had to stifle a laugh. A smile broke out on my face despite myself. "Let's just hope the inside makes up for it."

The card read:

Kristen, I'm sorry. I messed up. I lied to you and didn't respect your choices. Give me a chance to make it up to you.

Yours, Vincent

"This is really sweet, Vincent." I took a whiff of the roses and savored the fresh fragrance. The gesture touched my heart but gifts could only go so far.

"I'm glad you like it." He smiled, his boyish grin making my insides mushy. "So what did you want to tell me earlier today? It sounded important."

I carefully put the items on the seat next to me and exhaled, gathering up the courage to tell him what I'd planned on saying. "I want to take a break."

His smile faded and his dark eyes studied me. "What kind of break?"

"A break from us."

"Temporary or permanent?"

"Temporary. For now at least. My life is too crazy at the moment and I'm sure you're really stressed out as well. It'll be good for both of us."

His gaze narrowed. "The only time I'm not stressed is when I'm with you."

I looked at him skeptically. "What about your work? You've seemed pretty worried about it the last few weeks."

"Work is work. I can manage it, especially when I'm thinking about you. It helps to have something to look forward to."

"I thought you said I was a distraction?"

"That was when my priorities were different. Seems so long ago. Now work is the distraction."

"And I'm your main concern now? Is it because of Marty?"

"It's because the way I feel about you. You're more than a concern. You're a part of my life."

"You've been so busy lately. I've hardly seen you. I don't feel like I've been that big of a part of your life."

I expected him to have some kind of charming response but instead, he bent down and casually slipped off each of his black loafers, leaving him in his black socks. He set his shoes near my feet. Then he started slipping off my flats.

"Uh, what are you doing?"

He managed to slip off one when I pulled my legs away.

"I sincerely hope that you're not expecting us to have sex on your couch. I know you're all for 'finishing what we started' but roses and a cute card aren't going to cut it."

His expression was unreadable. "Give me your feet. I want to show you something."

"What for?"

"Trust me."

Sensing he didn't intend for us to have sex, I gingerly scooched my legs back and offered him the foot with the remaining shoe. He gently removed it and inserted my feet in his loafers.

I felt the lingering warmth of his feet on my own. I looked down and was fascinated by the maleness of the shoe. The texture of the leather was smooth and glossy but the slight crease near the toes and various small nicks gave it a rough, unrefined edge. The shape narrowing sharply at the toes seemed to point forward like a general points his hand to rally an army's charge. I imagined Vincent wearing these in a variety of scenarios: walking to high-powered meetings, standing in front of a podium giving a company-wide speech, bending down to pick up a quarter. My drab flats looked feminine and dainty in comparison.

I wiggled my toes inside, probing the empty space between the inner lining and my feet. Although comfortable, the loafers were much too big for me. They might as well have been clown shoes.

"Now close your eyes for a moment."

I did as he asked, expecting further instructions. After an awkward minute of not receiving any, I opened my eyes.

Vincent looked at me expectantly. "Well?"

"Well what?"

"What do you feel?"

I wiggled my toes again. "Umm . . . a soft insole? I don't know. What am I supposed to feel?"

"You're supposed to feel the muscles in your legs tensing, blood coursing between them, your cock getting hard like steel."

"Um, what?"

"You experience an intense attraction to Kristen. You were thinking about product strategy before but now your thoughts are turning dirty. You can't think straight. All you can think about is when you're going to see Kristen again. And if anyone hurts her, there will be hell to pay. Then you realize she's what you want. All you've ever wanted." He put his hand on my leg, the warmth seeping through the denim to my skin. "When you put yourself in my shoes. That's what you feel."

"Oh."

"Now imagine feeling that all the time. During meetings; on the plane; while you're eating . . . You see now how you're a part of my life?"

I nodded. "You make a good point."

"Do you still want to see me?"

Vincent's charm was starting to take its effect on me but I still had reservations. Maybe I'd built up resistance to him from all our time together. "I don't know. Yes and no."

"What are the reasons for 'yes'?"

I put my finger on my chin and thought about it. "You make a mean omelette."

"That's it?"

"Umm . . . Shrimp pasta as well. Also, you've shown you really care about me. Taking me on trips, carving time out of your busy schedule to be with me, being concerned about my safety."

"And the orgasms?"

"They're a nice perk but I think I could go without them and be okay."

"Then I have room for improvement. Okay, what are the reasons for 'no'?"

"I don't know if I can trust you."

"You've trusted me in the past."

"That's true."

"The bar in Cape Town, surfing, being discreet about our dating, blindfolds, cybersex, sex on my plane . . . am I missing anything?"

"Not that I can think of."

"And I messed up by getting that security team. And for not telling you about Giselle's ex-boyfriend, which you must admit is not a complete breach in trust. More like a half-breach."

I mused about it. "All right, I'll give you that."

"Also the Ariel text message was a misunderstanding so that doesn't count."

"It pissed me off so I'd say that's a half-breach."

"Fine. Even so, it's six in support of trusting me versus two in support of distrusting me. I'd say the odds are in my favor."

"In terms of numbers, maybe. But numbers are soft when there's feelings involved."

"Do you still have feelings for me?"

"Yes. I do. But I still think we should take a break."

He tried inserting his feet into my flats but only managed to squeeze a few toes inside.

"That's not what your shoes are telling me."

"Oh?" I became curious. "What are they saying?"

"They're saying life is crazy right now. I don't know what to do. I want to figure things out on my own because I'm a strong, independent woman. I want to prove it to Vincent and to myself. But I do know that Vincent really cares about me. He's always had the best intentions for me. And I really care about him. As much as I try to say otherwise, I really don't want to be apart from him."

I laughed despite myself, tears welling up in my eyes. He was so sweet. "My shoes talk too much."

He smiled and cleared his throat, but I could tell he was affected too, his eyes betraying him with a glisten. "Come on Kristen, give us a chance. We both have crazy lives but it doesn't mean we should fix things by ourselves. It might be easier. But if we make it through this together, we'll be stronger. If we make it through this alone, we'll just be better at being alone." He touched my cheek tenderly. "Let's work this out together."

He gently brought my head into his chest. I grumbled but didn't resist because it felt too good, too comforting. The distress I felt over our issues seemed to magically disappear when he held me. I realized how much I loved his touch and being with him despite our problems. It was worth taking a chance. Vincent was worth it. Even if it meant risking getting hurt.

"Fine," I muttered. "We'll do this together."

He exhaled in relief and kissed my head. "Can I call you Kitten again?" he asked, nuzzling his cheek in my hair.

I tried to think of a response that didn't make it seem like I totally forgave him. "As long as you let me call you Vinnie the Pooh."

He laughed, the throaty sound flowing over me. "That's the first time I've heard that one."

I looked up at him. "What other ones have you heard?"

"Vin Diesel. My Cousin Vinny. Vitty Cent. Vincent van Gogh . . ." He started grinning.

I giggled. "Those are pretty good but I think your drawing skills need a little work for that last one to work."

"You got me." He smiled. "I made that one up a while ago and tried to get people to use it but it never caught on."

I giggled again.

"But none of those names were as clever as yours." He bent and sealed his lips over my mouth. Our tongues slowly, tenderly probed one another until the need to breathe interrupted them. "You can call me whatever you like."

"I'll probably stick with 'Vincent'. I think it suits you best."

"Vincent it is then, Kitten. Listen, my sister Giselle is having a birthday party for her son next Saturday. Do you want to come with me?"

Vincent at a birthday party for his nephew? I had to see this. It would also give me the chance to meet his sister, Giselle. I recalled the picture he had of her in his island cabin, the two of them smiling on a beach together. I hadn't met any of Vincent's family before and I was more than curious to see how he would act around his sister.

"Sure. Am I going to see you before that this week?"

His face softened. "Not this week, sorry. Flying out tomorrow morning until Friday. I will call you every night, though. My schedule can slow down, Kristen, and it will. It's just going to take some time."

"Okay. I'll look forward to those calls, then."

"Me too."

Chapter Three

Sure enough, he called me every evening that week. The work week was otherwise pretty boring—fleshing out Vincent's BRIC strategy and continuing research on Selena Devries—but I began to look forward to talking to him every night so much that the days flew by. I appreciated that Vincent was making an effort after the events the previous weekend. Seeing the way he had been so violent with Marty had shaken my confidence in him, but his tender side was still there. It would be interesting to see how this would continue at his nephew's party.

Saturday morning finally came. Vincent picked me up from my apartment in a silver Aston Martin at nine in the morning. Traffic getting out of the city was a drag, as usual, but we spent the time chatting idly. It was an important step for us to build our relationship back up after it had been badly shaken with our fight. The whole day was important for that reason.

We arrived a little after ten-thirty and pulled up in front of a tidy suburban ranch-style home. The lawn was freshly mowed, and there were balloons on the mailbox announcing a birthday party. We parked on the street. Vincent had brought a birthday present wrapped in balloon wrapping paper, and I handed it to him as we got out of the car. We walked down the street and up the driveway to the house.

"So your nephew's name is Brady?" I asked Vincent, reading the sign on the mailbox.

Vincent smiled and grabbed my hand. The present was in the other. "Yup. He's turning three today."

"Did you pick out his present, or did your secretary Lucy?"

He scoffed. "I would never delegate such an august task. I picked this sucker out online months ago."

His mock offense at my question surprised me. "What is it?"

"This awesome train," he said enthusiastically. "The TrackMaster 500X. It makes twelve different sounds and has an automatic headlight for tunnels."

"Tunnels?"

"Blanket forts, tunnels, wherever it's dark. Point is, the kid's going to be an engineer like his uncle. He *loves* trains."

I nodded. Vincent was very enthused about this party, especially blanket forts. To be fair, I remembered loving making blanket forts as a kid. My inner child was in line with his inner child on that point.

"Who wrapped the present?" I asked, eyeing the perfect bows.

He laughed. "You caught me. That task I did delegate. It looks good though, right?"

I nodded. "Yeah, I think she deserves a bonus."

"I'll take it under consideration."

We made it to the porch, where we were already able to hear the high-pitched screams of a child running around and playing. The door was unlocked and Vincent stepped inside the house unfazed by the noise. I followed after.

We were greeted in the foyer by a blond, slim woman standing around five six. She had her hair tied back in a simple bun and wore a well-fitting dark blue blouse with black pants. By my first impression, she looked slightly younger than Vincent. I eyed the plate of snacks she was carrying: apple slices with peanut butter. My stomach growled.

"Hello, stranger," she said, smiling at her brother. Her voice was warm and confident. I could see the resemblance between her and Vincent both in appearance and in the confident way she carried herself.

After beaming at her brother for a moment, she turned to me. "And you must be Kristen."

She extended her hand and I took it. Her handshake was firm. "You're Giselle."

She smiled warmly. "As well as 'Mommy' and 'Mrs. Harper.' I'm glad you two could make it."

"Wouldn't miss it for the world," Vincent said.

The child causing all of the noise behind Giselle spotted us. His dark brown eyes opened wide and he tottered over wearing his cone-shaped birthday hat, followed by a man with black hair and a bright smile. "Uncle Vincent!"

Vincent squatted down on his heels and gave Brady a big hug as the man following him took his place beside Giselle. Seeing Vincent in his blue jeans and white polo shirt in this family setting revealed a new side of him. "Hey buddy, how's it going?"

"It's my birthday!" Brady apparently hadn't quite learned volume control yet.

Vincent didn't even flinch at his nephew's high-pitched screaming. "I know. I got you a present!"

The boy screamed in delight. The little guy was super cute and very excited, if a little loud.

Vincent stood back up and shook hands with what I assumed was Giselle's husband, eyeing him firmly. "Good morning, Rob."

Rob returned the gesture. "Vincent."

Vincent put his arm around me. "Rob, this is my girlfriend Kristen. Kristen, this is Giselle's husband Rob."

"Good to meet you," Rob said. He had kind, gray eyes, and looked to be a similar age to Giselle. His build was smaller than Vincent's, but I thought he and Giselle made a cute couple.

Rob reached down and patted Brady on the back. "Brady, this is Kristen. Say hello."

Brady ran up and wrapped his arms around my leg, gripping the fabric of my jeans. "Hi Kristen."

Brady was too cute. I squatted down as Vincent had. "How old are you?" I asked him. I wanted to show Vincent that I was comfortable with children too.

Brady looked at Giselle and then back at me.

"Tell him how old you are, Brady," Giselle said.

He looked at me a little longer and appeared to decide I was okay, to my relief. "I'm three," he squealed.

"Good job!" Giselle said.

Emboldened, he grabbed my hand. His cute little fingers wrapped around one of mine. "Let's go play trains!" he said enthusiastically.

I smiled and followed him. Vincent stayed behind to talk to his sister and brother-in-law.

As Brady led me to his play area, I looked around at the house and all the little touches Giselle had put on her home. Lamps, candles, vases, mirrors: everything was in good taste and combined attractively. It was hard to imagine a life where managing the household was a significant part of what you thought about. Riley and I looked after ourselves, but we were pretty low-maintenance and kept decorating simple.

When we got to his play area, the floor was littered with an array of trains, train track decorations, and even a stuffed conductor. A train track in a big figure eight was spread amidst the chaos. Vincent was right: Brady loved trains. As clean as the rest of the house was, Giselle had clearly decided that Brady's play area was a place where messiness could reign.

I got down on my knees to be down on Brady's eye level. He eyed me earnestly. "Which one?" he asked.

Scanning the floor, I took a red train in my hand and put it on the track. Brady hit the switch on the control center at the track's control house and the train zoomed around. He laughed approvingly.

"Which one for you?" I asked him.

In response, he got up and ran over to a shelf where a child-sized blue conductor cap was hanging on a hook. He picked it up and threw it sloppily on his head before tottering back over. He plopped down next to me and picked a black train to put on the track.

Brady wanted to play with me, but once he started he was in his own little world, watching the trains. After a minute of watching him I heard a familiar voice behind me.

"I got him that cap," Vincent said. He took a seat next to me and watched Brady maneuver his train in silence. A warm smile was on his face the entire time.

Brady played with his train for a while longer before he noticed Vincent had taken a seat at the play area. When he saw Vincent at last, his brown eyes lit up anew.

"Uncle Vincent! Which one?"

Vincent picked out a yellow train to add to the track. Whether it was the train track itself or playing with Brady, he was enjoying this moment in a playful way that I hadn't seen before.

"Hey buddy," Vincent said after a moment, "why don't we build a tunnel for our trains?"

"Yeah!" Brady yelled.

I watched as Vincent got a chair from another room and returned with a blanket. He put the chair at one end of the figure eight, and Brady helped him with the blanket as well as he could. Soon they were racing the trains under their makeshift tunnel.

Brady's enthusiasm for the whole activity was infectious. I could tell Vincent was getting into it, and soon enough so was I, watching the trains fly by faster and faster. Vincent was in the middle of talking to Brady about changing the track to take better advantage of the chair when Giselle came into the room.

"Looks like you guys are having a blast," she said.

Brady was very excited. "Trains!" he yelled.

"I see that. Kristen, do you want to help me finish frosting the C-A-K-E? I think the boys are occupied for a while and Rob just went out to grab some last minute party supplies before Brady's friends come over."

I looked up and sensed a hint of seriousness beneath her innocent veneer. "Of course," I said. "You two will be okay without me, right?"

Vincent looked up from instigating a train crash. "I think so." Brady was too engrossed to notice us.

"Okay," I said. "Be back soon." With that, I got up and followed Giselle into the kitchen.

Giselle's kitchen was a total disaster, which was to be expected when you were throwing a birthday party for a three-year old. Various kitchen implements were strewn across the granite countertop, and a metallic mixing bowl was sitting next to a fresh and delicious smelling round yellow cake. She walked over to the bowl and began stirring the contents inside.

"Have you ever baked a cake before?" she asked over her shoulder.

I wasn't very good in the kitchen. It was one of my failings: I had always been too busy with school and then work to learn how to cook well. I was mostly good with a microwave and doing basic things on a stove top, like warming up soup. Baking a cake from scratch was beyond me.

"Not on my own, no," I said. "The most I've done is bake a cake out of a box with my mother, but that was years ago."

She flashed a quick smile over her shoulder as she whisked the frosting. "Neither had I, until I had to bake a cake for Brady's first birthday. It was hilariously lop-sided, but thankfully one-year olds don't notice that kind of thing."

"It looks like you've gotten pretty good," I said.

"I'm trying, anyway." She waved me over. "Well, even if you haven't done this before, I'm sure you can give it a go. Just try and coat this evenly with frosting. I'm going to work on the blue frosting for writing happy birthday."

I took the plastic frosting spreader from its place on the counter and went to work. It wasn't very different from spreading peanut butter and jelly on a sandwich, which I was a pro at. I quickly got into a rhythm of taking a gob of frosting and smoothing it out on the cake.

Giselle watched me work for a moment and then set to work on the colored frosting. "So you've been seeing Vincent for a little while now?" she asked.

"That's right."

"How did you two meet?"

I laughed nervously. Apparently Vincent hadn't told her much. I decided to be truthful since the cat was out of the bag anyway. "To be honest, it's a bit scandalous."

She stopped whisking. "You weren't married or something, were you?"

"No!" I cried. "Why? Do you think Vincent would do something like that?"

"I don't, but people have a way of surprising you sometimes."

I knew all about that, but I had forgotten what Vincent told me about her history. I wondered if he had told her about the situation with Marty. That was a private thing: the only people who knew about it were Vincent and Riley. Well, and Kurt and Bernie. It still upset me that he had done that. *That* had surprised me. As sweet as he had been all week, I still wasn't over it.

"I guess that's true," I said. "Anyway, we actually met through work. I work for a personal wealth management firm and head up his account."

She turned and looked at me. "Good for you! I hope you're reining him in somewhat. Every time he travels I worry he's going to have some horrible accident with all the risky sports he's doing."

"Oh, you too?"

She let out a short laugh and shook her head. "He seems to like you. I haven't met a girlfriend of his before."

Here was another surprise. The fact that Vincent had never introduced a girlfriend to his sister, who he was obviously close to, made me feel special. My mind shot to Ariel Diamond. If his sister had never met her, maybe things weren't as serious between them as I had thought, even if the tattoo was strange.

"Not even Ariel?" I asked, before I knew the words were out of my mouth.

Giselle stopped whisking the frosting for a moment, but continued. "No, not Ariel. That was a different period in Vincent's life. And mine, really. We didn't talk much while he was dating her."

"I see."

"He's much more family oriented now than he was then."

"Oh?"

"Ever since our parents died. He grew up after that."

I stopped in place. Vincent's parents were dead? He had never talked about them, but then I rarely talked about my parents and they were still alive and kicking back in Texas. How had it never come up that his parents had already passed away? Did he just not care?

I began spreading the frosting again. "I didn't know your parents had passed," I said quietly.

It was her turn to put her whisk down. "Oh, sorry. I guess it's been so long. They passed away nine years ago."

So Vincent must have been very young. Younger than I was as I stood in that kitchen. Even though I didn't talk to my parents much and didn't rely on them financially at all, I couldn't imagine them being gone.

"Wow, you two were young then."

"I like to think thirty is still young!" she said, laughing.

My cheeks flushed. "That's not what I meant!"

"I know, I know. It was way too young to lose our parents. Vincent took it very hard. It actually turned out to be the beginning of his success."

"What do you mean?"

"After they passed away, he finally got his act together. He developed the camera a few months after the funeral. It was like he was possessed. We were both staying at our parents' house for awhile after the accident and living on the small inheritance we got. He would be working twenty hours a day for weeks on end, out in the garage and on the computer and on the phone. It was a transformation. He went from being a slacker with potential to someone who was totally obsessed."

The tone in her voice had changed. Her words took on a strange sharpness, like she was trying to cut them into me and make sure they sunk in. She obviously admired Vincent very deeply. This wasn't a connection that was for the sake of appearances: Vincent meant the world to her. Listening to her talk about him, I could see why.

She continued. "Any time he wasn't working he was saying he was going to take care of me and of us. To a twenty year old it's pretty weird to have your surfer brother tell you that he's going to take care of the family. It sounds like wishful thinking from a guy who's just grieving for his parents, but Vincent really changed. He became this very intense person who found success everywhere he looked because he wouldn't accept failure. He was selling that camera in three months and had it with retailers soon after, and he just built and built. Everyone underestimates him because of his appearance and his hobbies, but he just keeps plowing forward."

I had researched the story of Vincent's company from a financial perspective, but I hadn't given thought to what it meant on a personal level to grind out so much success. Giselle had seen it first hand. In a way, I was almost jealous.

"It sounds like you admire him," I said, simply because I hadn't spoken in a while. We had both stopped with our frosting duties.

She nodded. "Then he changed again when Brady was born. Before that, he was on a path where it was nothing but business and intensity, but you can't be intense with a newborn. Vincent makes sure my son has the best of everything. Vincent set up Brady's college fund the day after Brady was born, and has done so much research on camps and things to send him to."

She shrugged, laughing. "I'll get these emails at two a.m. saying 'it's your kid but I just want to tell you I'm happy to pay to send him to this camp when he's old enough' or 'do you think Brady would like this? I can get it delivered this weekend.' Never mind my son, it's a full-time job keeping up with Vincent!"

Before today, I would've had a hard time imagining Vincent being so focused on a child. He was always so busy either with his business or doing crazy recreational activities. Having a kid was a lot of responsibility. It was almost in complete opposition to his lifestyle. "It sounds like he practically treats Brady as his own kid."

She shook her head. "He knows the limit. The way he gives me options is always a one-off. He doesn't argue with me or nag me or anything like that. He cares tremendously about his nephew and has an unusual capacity for helping out, so he's taking advantage of that. Plus as you've seen, his gifts for Brady aren't outrageous. I think Brady will become conscious of how much money his uncle has very slowly." She took a taste of the frosting. "Put it this way: it's a good parenting challenge to have."

"What does Rob think?"

"He's supportive. Vincent and him get along well. My brother takes the protective older sibling thing very seriously."

I knew more about how protective Vincent could be than I wanted to. "I bet."

Giselle turned and looked at me intently. I did my best to keep a poker face and concentrate on spreading the frosting, though I could see her out of the corner of my eye. To my relief, she finally went back to her own frosting job.

"Anyway," she said, "Vincent's wonderful with Brady. Like another child. I hope he can have children of his own soon."

I dropped the frosting spreader on the counter and it tumbled to the floor. Embarrassed, I scrambled and picked it up. Was she suggesting what I thought she was?

She stopped whisking again and squinted, smiling quizzically. "I didn't say he's in a rush!"

I washed it off in the sink before wiping up the frosting on the floor. "Sorry, I'm just a little clumsy."

She stood with her arms crossed, watching me again. "That's okay, accidents happen."

Her sleeves were rolled up, and as I was looking at her trying to judge her expression my eyes fell to some peculiar scars on her forearms. Were those cigarette burns? Nothing in the house smelled like cigarette smoke, so I was guessing she wasn't a smoker. Maybe she had been one in the past, before Brady. Or maybe it was something more nefarious.

She seemed to notice I was looking at her arms and rolled down her sleeves before turning back to work. "Anyway, I do hope things work out between you two," Giselle said. "I would love it if Vincent has finally found someone to share his life with."

I let the question of her arms go and flashed a smile fit for a job interview. "So far he's been pretty great."

I heard their footsteps a second before they burst in. There was a crash at the kitchen door, then the knob turned and Brady came in giggling, with Vincent close behind.

"Hey buddy, come back. Where are you going?" Vincent cried.

Brady made a beeline straight for me and threw his arms around my right leg. "Kristen," he screamed, "Come play trains!"

I looked at Giselle, who was smiling. "It looks like I'm being summoned," I said.

"I think so. You guys have fun, I can finish up here."

The three of us went back and played trains until the cake was ready. By that point, a couple of Brady's friends had come over with their parents, and Vincent and I were nearly forgotten. The party ended up lasting until seven o'clock. By the time we left, I was as tuckered out as the kids. I slept in the car the whole way home.

Chapter Four

Sunday was a blur of errands and getting my life in order. Seeing Vincent in a family environment was a serious eye-opener. After the way he had handled Marty, I was afraid I was dating a hyper-logical man with the emotions of a caveman. But now, seeing him with Brady, it was clear he had a lot of love in his heart. That made me feel good.

Monday morning I dragged my feet out of bed and lurched my way to work. As I stepped off the elevator on the forty-eighth floor of the tall, glass building housing Waterbridge-Howser, I started feeling dizzy. I had a rough night trying to sleep and only ended up getting a few hours. When I got to my office, I put down my bag and walked right back out. I needed caffeine. Badly.

I went to the common kitchen area with my cup. When I smelled the coffee pot, it made me nauseous.

"Man, who made the coffee this morning? It smells terrible."

An analyst named Sam was also in the kitchen; he was busy slathering a bagel with cream cheese. He took a bite of his bagel then a sip of his mug. "Hmm tastes fine to me. I don't smell anything unusual."

"You don't smell it? It smells like dirty feet and tires."

"Maybe you got a super sniffer."

"A what?"

"You know, like someone who has super sensitive taste buds except with smell. I saw it on an episode of Law & Order. When the police dog was unable to sniff out drugs from a crime scene, they brought in this guy who was a super sniffer."

Suddenly curious that I might have a superpower, I asked, "Did he find anything at the scene?"

He nodded vigorously. "He sniffed out this scent that the dog wasn't trained to detect. It was some weird chemical that led the police to this abandoned paint factory where they found incriminating evidence."

"Interesting."

"See if you can sniff my deodorant." He lifted up his armpit and I noticed a faint sweat stain on the shirt fabric. Fortunately he was several feet away.

"I can't smell anything from here."

"Maybe you're not a super sniffer then."

"Yeah, I don't think I have that ability. Otherwise, I would've probably figured it out earlier."

He took another bite of his bagel. "Could be you're pregnant."

I nearly dropped my empty mug but caught it at the last moment. "What?"

He finished chewing. "When my wife was pregnant, she couldn't stand certain smells. Like coffee and the smell of the grocery store."

I laughed nervously and batted my hand at the notion. Sam shrugged and went off to his own desk to do work or perhaps ponder the mystery.

I remained in the kitchen. What if I really was pregnant?

The past couple weeks raced through my mind. I'd vomited twice. The first time I'd attributed to bad Chinese food. The second time happened because I was distraught over Marty showing up and the argument with Vincent that followed. Surely it wasn't morning sickness . . .

My hand flew to cover my open mouth when I realized something: it was almost a week now that my period was late.

Oh no.

During lunch, I made a trip to Duane Reade and picked up a pregnancy test. When I got to the family planning aisle, I felt like I was walking into a sex shop looking over my shoulder every second like I was about to do something scandalous. I found what I was looking for and tucked the box under my arm until I reached the register. After paying, I hurriedly put the box in my purse hoping no one saw me buy it.

When I got home, I spotted Riley in her usual spot on the couch watching TV. I set down my tote in a kitchen chair and headed for the bathroom with the test box in hand, careful to keep it hidden from Riley.

I locked the door and stared at the box for a moment. The picture on the front showed a woman smiling brightly. I glanced in the mirror and saw that my expression looked nothing like that.

I took out a strip and followed the directions, my hands trembling the entire time.

It would take a few minutes before the results showed. I closed my eyes and started a countdown in my mind, dreading to see the result.

Deep breaths, Kristen.

Finally, five minutes had passed. I looked down at the test in my hand.

Pink line. I was pregnant.

I dropped the test on the floor. My hands were shaking. This had to be a mistake. No way I was pregnant. I'd been on birth control. Even though Vincent came inside me when we were in the Caribbean, there was no way he got me pregnant. It didn't matter how potent his sperm was, it couldn't beat birth control . . . right?

I took another one.

Five excruciatingly long minutes later, I looked at it.

Pink line again.

Shit. Shit shit shit. Shit. Fuck.

My world was coming apart. *This can't be happening.*

I frantically examined the box, hoping to find a warning about its inaccuracy.

"Over 99% accurate. Take comfort in knowing your results."

I stepped out of the bathroom and went to the living room where Riley was sipping a diet coke.

"Riley, I need to ask you something." I tried to keep my voice as calm as possible for someone who just discovered they were pregnant.

She put her drink down on the coffee table and turned her attention to me. "Sure, what is it?"

"Is it possible to get two false-positives on a pregnancy test?"

"Huh? Why are you . . ." Her eyes widened. "Oh my god. Are you pregnant?"

I tried holding the tears back but they started flowing against my will. "I just took a test and that's what it said."

"I thought you were on birth control!"

"I was, I mean, I am. I just—I don't know how this could have happened."

"Oh Kris, you know that even the pill isn't one-hundred percent effective."

I nodded. "I mean, I knew that as a concept, but I never thought that I'd be the tiny sliver of a percentage that it would fail for!"

Riley studied my face, probably discerning that congratulations weren't in order. Her tone became serious. "What are you going to do?"

I started crying harder. "I never planned for this. Vincent and I never talked about it. We've barely even known each other for two months!"

Riley came to hug me and rub my back. "It's going to be okay, Kris. You have options. It's not the end of the world."

"I don't know what to do."

Her voice was soft. "Are you considering getting an abortion?"

"I don't know. What other choice do I have? I'm not ready to be a mom. I thought I'd be into my thirties before I considered having a baby. I don't even know how Vincent would react if he found out."

"Are you going to tell him?"

"Should I?"

"You should. He has a right to know. He is the father right?"

I wiped the tears from my cheek. "Unless my fingers have started magically producing sperm, yes. Vincent's the only one I've had sex with."

"Okay. How is your relationship with him going? You said you two made up right?"

"Yeah, we did."

"Good. That should make it easier to tell him. Have faith in him, Kris. Didn't you say he adored his nephew?"

Giselle's stories about Vincent's emails in the early morning hours enthusing over activities and programs for Brady ran through my mind. "He does. I think he might actually be too intense about it."

"What do you mean?"

"I don't know, his sister made it sound like he's borderline obsessed with the kid. Sends her emails at two in the morning with camps and stuff his nephew can go to when he's old enough."

Riley nodded. "That sounds very sweet. It sounds like he would be a great dad."

"I don't know Riley, liking kids is not the same as wanting one of your own."

"That's true. He's a busy CEO and lives a fast-paced lifestyle. But liking kids is certainly a positive sign."

"Or what if he really does want a child and I don't? What if I just don't want to be a mom yet? I could get an abortion and not tell him. Wouldn't that be easier? If I tell him, and we disagree, this could destroy our relationship. Then it would have been easier just to not tell him, and maybe we can have a baby years from now."

She sucked in a deep breath. "I think you should think hard about whether you want to get an abortion. My mother had an unplanned pregnancy and almost got an abortion. I'm glad she didn't, otherwise I wouldn't be here."

I could feel my face grow hot with embarrassment. "Riley, I didn't know . . ."

"It's okay. We all have secrets Kristen." She squeezed my hand. "Just don't make a quick decision. Think about it. I think I would tell Vincent. If you make this decision by yourself, it's going to be a strain on your relationship for the rest of the time you're together. I mean, it's pretty dishonest."

She made a good point. If Vincent couldn't trust me to talk to him about something this important, that said bad things about the health of our relationship as a whole. Still though, it was just so much to deal with. "You don't think I'm too young to have a child?"

Riley shook her head. "You're twenty-five. A lot of women have children at that age. When people are as young as we are, typically money is a big concern, but that's obviously not the case here. You have a great job and Vincent is loaded."

"That's part of it though, Riley. I can't have a baby fathered by my client. That's beyond scandalous. If I decide to have this baby, my time at Waterbridge-Howser is done."

"I thought you said they had no policy against it!"

I sighed. "Official policy is one thing. Shoving it in the company's face by taking maternity leave to have a baby fathered by a client is another. It's practically proof they got the client because I had sex with him. Other wealth management firms could use that against them every time they make a pitch. The wealth management business is pretty conservative."

"So they would fire you? Isn't that illegal?"

"They might if they could figure out how to get away with it, or they would force me out slowly. It doesn't matter. If I decide to have this baby, I need to find a new job before it happens. Before I start showing, actually."

"Wow. That is a lot to handle."

"It feels like too much. What is Vincent going to say when I drop all these problems on his lap?"

She shook her head. "Talk to him and find out. He's the CEO of an enormous company, I'm sure he's used to dealing with complicated situations. If you don't talk to him about it, I think you'll regret it later."

"And if we break up because we can't work it out?"

"If you guys can't work through an issue like this together, is the relationship still worth it?"

I took a deep breath. "I guess not. Still though. This is so much."

"You don't have to make a decision yet. Like I said, I think you should talk to him. That's what I would do."

That night, I lay in bed thinking about how chaotic my life had become. I was pregnant. It explained how strange I had been feeling lately, but it still left me with more questions than answers. My life had been on the straight and narrow for so long, traveling steadily along a single path. The past two months had been the sharpest detour I could imagine.

Vincent was part of that detour, though, and the more I thought about it, the more I agreed with Riley. I needed to talk to him about my pregnancy. It was unplanned, yes, but maybe it would end up being a pleasant accident. I couldn't rule that out. What I did know was if I made the decision without keeping him in the loop, I would have to hide that from him for the rest of my life. As long as we were together, anyway. I didn't want that hanging over our relationship.

I had a meeting scheduled with him on Thursday. So far, the topic of the meeting would be going over the investment strategy options I had developed for his personal wealth, but it looked like there would be another item added to the agenda, official or not.

Chapter Five

Tuesday and Wednesday passed by in a blur of anxiety. Most of that time had been spent on thinking about the pregnancy than on actual work. I'd wavered back and forth between wanting to tell Vincent and not wanting to tell him, wanting to keep the baby and not wanting to keep the baby.

By the time Thursday came, I'd made up my mind that I was going to tell Vincent, but I was still unsure about my personal stance on keeping the baby or not. I would need to know how Vincent felt before making a decision on how I felt.

Work before the meeting with Vincent was a morass of emails and memos. I kept having to reread messages to make sure I hadn't missed anything. It was impossible to focus; I couldn't tell if it was hormones or nervousness, but my mind felt dull and fuzzy. Even though I would have usually completed the work in thirty minutes, it took a full four hours before it was done.

Finally, the moment came for me to leave for my meeting. I packed up my stuff and took a cab over to his office. The ride went by in a numb haze. How would I start the conversation? How would he react, regardless of how I started it? The course of my life could depend on this meeting. Funny how it's always the people you least expect that end up changing your life in the biggest ways. A few months ago, I would have never thought I'd have Vincent Sorenson's unborn child nestled in my womb, but here I was.

I took a deep breath and exited the cab. The walk from the curb into his building and up the elevator felt like a sprint. I was going to do this. Striding through the Red Fusion office, I waved to his secretary before reaching his office. His door was half open and I knocked on it.

"Come in," Vincent called.

I eased the door open and walked through. Vincent wasn't sitting at his desk. Rather, he was looking out the window, lost in thought. He wore a slim cut pair of navy pants and a white and light blue checkered shirt separated by a tan leather belt. Casual but neat. I still wasn't used to how sexy he looked in whatever he wore.

He turned over his shoulder and looked at me. "Hello, Kristen. You're a few minutes early."

"Am I?" I asked. I looked at my watch. "Sorry about that. Traffic was lighter than expected."

He waved his hand as if pushing aside my words and smiled. "Don't worry, it's a good surprise. I like good surprises. "

He took a couple steps toward where I was standing just inside his door. "Close that," he said.

I knew that tone. He was seconds away from kissing me, and if that started, there was no way I was going to end up talking to him about the pregnancy. I held up the file I had prepared for presenting the strategy I had in mind for his assets. "We should get through this," I said. "It is important, after all. I also have something else to tell you afterwards, something unrelated to business."

"It must be about pleasure then. I'm looking forward to it, Kitten."

I smiled but inwardly resisted letting his usual effect on me take hold. Vincent didn't need any extra encouragement to keep teasing me and I didn't need him trying to derail my carefully laid plan.

"Not quite, let's just take it one thing at a time."

He sighed. "You're right. Where do you want me?"

In context it sounded sexual and my sex instinctively tightened at his tone. With how busy he'd been the past few weeks and the crazy events that happened, it seemed like forever since we had sex. I needed to focus. One thing at a time. *First get through your presentation and then you can tell him about the baby.*

He cocked an eyebrow. "Are you okay?"

I shook my head. "Yes, sorry. I was just thinking about my presentation."

He laughed. "I hope you're not as nervous as you were the first time we were in this office. Though I rather enjoyed that conversation . . . "

Even though he got a smile out of me, I knew I had to get this discussion back on track. "Sorry Vincent, don't think that's happening today."

"Okay, well once you're done presenting these materials maybe we can move on to phase two of the meeting."

Vincent clearly had a different idea of how phase two of the meeting was going to go.

"We can just sit on the couch," I said.

How would he react when he found out about the baby? It was clear from our weekend visit with Giselle that Vincent loved Brady, but that was his nephew. He didn't have to take care of Brady every day. Would he feel the same way if the child was his? Would he be willing to sacrifice his lifestyle for that?

He took a seat. "I hope I can have your undivided attention here," he said. "Otherwise I'll have to make sure."

Lewd images of the different ways he'd "make sure" flashed in my mind before I took a deep breath and smiled up at him. "Sorry, I'm just preoccupied with some things at work."

Hopefully a discussion of the facts and figures of his wealth would deflate things. I handed him the binder I had put together for this presentation.

He smiled at me. I waited for him to speak, but he continued to watch me, saying nothing.

I blinked and plowed ahead, opening the binder and turning past the cover page to the executive summary. I launched into an explanation of the different strategies we had prepared for him.

He nodded, attentive, though there was also still a knowing smirk on his face.

"Any questions so far?" I asked.

He shook his head, pursing his lips as if to avoid smiling.

"What's so funny?"

He looked at me a few beats. Still fighting back a smile, he finally spoke. "Are you listening to yourself?"

I scrunched my face. What was he talking about? "Did I say something wrong?"

"No, you've been doing fine. It's just . . ." He trailed off.

"What?"

Then I heard it. I had the tiny rasp I sometimes got in my voice when I was turned on.

I cleared my throat then pursed my lips, trying to think of what to say. This was not going to plan. Not my plan anyway, though Vincent seemed to be enjoying himself. Damn these pregnancy hormones.

"Vincent, this is important."

"Do you know how you look right now?" Vincent's eyes flickered up and down my body, I could almost feel his invisible fingers caressing my curves slowly. His tongue darted out and wet his lips slightly.

"You should see yourself in a mirror, you look too fuckable. I could just tear your clothes off right now. It's been too long. We both know we're far overdue for sex."

The desire in his voice sent a spike of heat to my core. I squirmed, rubbing my legs together. For some reason, I thought about the first time I was here in his office. We were right here on his couch. Except we were lying down, not sitting, and his hands had been sliding up my thigh. I looked at him and blushed, hoping that he couldn't read my mind. I needed to get this back on track.

"Don't you care about managing your assets?"

He moved closer to me, his leg pressing right up against mine. It was good that we were sitting down, because looking into his deep brown eyes, I felt ready to melt. He lifted his right hand, gliding the back of his fingers down the side of my face.

"You're my most valuable asset right now," he whispered.

A shiver ran down the back of my spine. He was being so sweet and it was getting more difficult by the minute to resist him.

"I'm serious, Vincent."

He closed the binder and set it down on the glass coffee table. "Listen, I trust the strategy you've put together for me, and I'm sure I can read through this on my own when I'm less distracted. We don't need to decide on a strategy right this minute."

Vincent turned back to me, a fire burning in his eyes. He caressed my hair with one hand, moving down my tender exposed neck, and with his other gripped my bare leg possessively. I closed my eyes, delighting in the sensations for a moment.

"What if someone hears us?" I whispered.

"These glass walls could stop bullets. No one will hear us."

"Vincent."

"Kitten, I've wanted to take you in this office since the first time you were here."

"There's something I need to tell you . . ."

"Shhh . . . it can wait. I can't."

Who knew what would happen between us after he learned about the pregnancy. I decided I could wait a little longer to tell him so that we could enjoy each other's bodies, in this moment. It might be the last time.

His mouth covered mine, claiming a kiss. My body betrayed me, responding to his touch like it belonged to him. I leaned back until I was lying down on the couch, Vincent's chest pressed against mine.

His fingers eased down toward my pussy, which was on fire. I arched my hips up to give him better access, desperate for him to touch me. He obliged and pressed against my soaked underwear.

"You're so wet for me, Kristen. Tell me where you want me now." He slid a finger around my panties and into my pussy, hitting the perfect spot. He massaged my tender spot slowly, drawing out my pleasure, as if he was demonstrating his control over my body.

It sent me over the edge. I came hard, biting the fabric of his shirt to stop from crying out. Bucking wildly, my muscles contracted in spasms that would have been painful if they didn't feel so earth shatteringly good. Vincent kept hold of me, his lone finger pulsing against my g-spot.

When I had finally finished, I eased up and saw I had left mascara on his shirt to go along with the color on my lips. Turning to his face, I saw a mixture of surprise and arousal in his expression.

He took his finger out of me and grabbed my hips. Looking up at me, he smiled wickedly. "You were ready, weren't you?"

I nodded. "Sorry about your shirt."

He looked over dismissively. "I have another. Do you?"

I looked at my blouse, but it was fine.

He squeezed my hips. In response, I kissed him desperately on the mouth. I loved it when he challenged me. He knew just which buttons to press and when. In this case, he had lit a new fire to go along with my already aching need.

I fumbled with the buttons on his shirt, my mouth still pressed against his. Finding the prize I had been looking for, I relished the sensations of his smooth chest, taut and hard. His nipple rings were polished and surprisingly warm under my hand.

"Kitten," he groaned. "I need to be inside you."

I nodded.

Vincent picked me up, flipping me over. I kneeled on the couch, turning my back to him. He slid his hand up my thigh, groping me possessively. God, I needed him inside me. I spread my legs wider for him, giving him better access, thrusting my needy sex closer towards him. The air felt cool against my skin, making me hyper aware of how exposed I was to him. I heard his belt unbuckle.

My body shuddered as he entered me. I clenched involuntarily around him as he dragged the turgid tip of his cock against my slick inner walls. I didn't know how much more I could take, the pleasure was too intense.

"Vincent, please . . . "

He continued to thrust into me, repeatedly hitting my pleasure center, until we shattered together. I felt him come inside me, his warm seed mixing with my fluids and I followed soon after, arching myself into the air, offering Vincent my body. Afterwards he collapsed on me and we laid there on the couch.

His weight on top of me was comforting. We breathed in sync, recovering slowly from our ecstasy. After he wiped the evidence of our encounter from my leg, we curled up together on the couch. We were both sweaty, but it felt good to have his warmth next to me.

It had to be now or it wasn't going to happen today. I needed to tell him I was pregnant. Now it was time to see how he was going to react. At least I knew he would be in the best possible mood.

I took a deep breath as my heart started beating faster in anticipation of the fallout. "Vincent—"

The intercom buzzed, sending my insides into freefall.

"Mr. Sorenson, security just called up. Mr. Rodriguez and Mr. Bennet are here for you. Shall I let them know you and Ms. Daley aren't finished?"

Vincent untangled himself from me and strode over to his desk. He tilted his head questioningly at me as if asking me if we were done. A loose strand of hair on his face, coupled with his dimpled smile gave him a boyish look.

I couldn't tell him. He—no—we were so happy in the moment, that I couldn't spoil it and drop this bomb on him just before leaving. The important part wasn't so much me telling him as his reaction, and leaving right after I told him wouldn't allow me to see that. With that in mind, I nodded quietly and straightened myself out.

"No Lucy, we're just wrapping up. I'll be down in a minute."

"I'll let them know."

"Thank you, Lucy."

He turned to me and the anxiety I had before the meeting returned. We needed to have a discussion about how to handle this, but it won't be right now. There will be other opportunities. I had at least a few more weeks before I had to make a final decision about the baby.

"Sorry about that, they're a little early. That's Kurt and Bernie, they're keeping tabs on Marty, just as a precaution. You can stay if you want to sit in."

I shook my head. "No, it's okay. I have to get back to work anyway."

Vincent watched me for a moment then shrugged. "I promise, I'll read through those materials tonight and we can talk about them."

"Thank you. Sorry we couldn't get through everything we needed to."

He smiled. "I think we found a better substitute for our time, don't you."

I returned the smile and continued to straighten out my hair.

He laughed quietly as he went to his closet and found a new dress shirt. "You're good to go, right?"

I was sure I looked a mess, but I could deal with it on my own time. "I'll stop in the ladies room before I head out."

He finished buttoning up. "Good as new," he said.

He opened the door to let me out first. He left, and I headed to the ladies room. Just as I entered, my phone buzzed. It was Riley:

How did the pregnancy convo with V go?

I texted back.

Interrupted. Will do it soon.

I leaned against the bathroom counter and let out a long sigh. It was just a little more time, that was all. I had weeks before I would be showing; surely I could find a good time before then. Missing this chance wasn't the end of the world.

***

That evening, when my head was clearer, I realized my mistake. While it was true that I didn't need to tell Vincent right away, I hadn't counted on the storm cloud hanging over my head every minute I didn't tell him.

After an hour of trying to distract myself with TV and cleaning, I decided that the sooner I told him the better. Vincent was too distracting in his office, dressed in his business attire, but maybe we'd both be more focused if we had the conversation at my place.

I called Vincent at his office and asked him to come over, telling him that I absolutely had to see him to talk to him about something. He sounded concerned and told me he would swing by in a couple hours. That done, I talked to Riley about having the apartment to myself for the evening. Good friend that she was, she called her friend Jen and was out for the night.

As I waited for Vincent to come by, I was determined that there would *definitely* not be a replay of what happened earlier that day in his office.

Chapter Six

On my way now. Be there in 10 mins.

After reading Vincent's text, I took a deep breath and set my phone down on the glass coffee table.

I started heating up water on the stove to make tea. It would help calm my nerves along with Vincent's during the delicate conversation. I sat on the couch rehearsing the lines I'd prepared to say to him as I smoothed out my t-shirt and jeans.

A few minutes later, a knock at the door startled me. Three raps followed by the faint sound of a man clearing his throat.

I got up from my seat and walked to the door. Looking through the peephole, I saw Vincent standing on my doormat. He was wearing a forest-green polo with sleeves that stretched against his arms and khaki shorts which showcased the taut muscles in his legs. He must've changed after work. He was shifting his feet, which betrayed his apprehension. Did he suspect what I was about to tell him?

I opened the door. "Hey," I said, pasting on the smile I'd prepared beforehand. It was easier once I saw his breathtaking face.

His expression brightened. "Hey," he said, smiling back at me.

"Come on in." I stepped back, pulling the door wider and gesturing him inside.

"Should I take off my shoes?"

He was wearing a clean pair of sneakers that matched his polo. I half-suspected he was probing me with the question. Telling him to leave his shoes on could be interpreted as a sign that I was breaking up with him. This was going to be a long conversation and he deserved to be comfortable.

"You can take them off."

He removed his shoes and set them carefully next to the pile of flats and heels in the corner near the coat rack.

"Would you like something to drink? I'm in the middle of making some tea." I studied his body language. He was slightly tense, his movements lacking the usual primal confidence.

"I'm fine, thank you."

The formality of his response made the situation even more awkward. "Okay." Once he was clear of the entrance, I leaned forward to close the door. The closing of the door would mark the beginning of a very difficult conversation.

Here goes.

The door made an unexpected thud as I tried to jam it shut. I glanced down and saw a dark brown boot wedged into the door frame.

Huh?

A dull, metallic chrome object slid through the narrow opening in the door. The shape was small and ended in a point—aimed at Vincent's back.

"Stay away from her!" the voice behind the door screamed.

A force pushed me. I staggered backward, my shoulder blades crashing against the half-wall separating the living room from the kitchen. The door flew open and a tall man with white bandages across his nose and cheeks entered my apartment. He was wearing a plain white t-shirt with black athletic pants and looked very pissed off.

Vincent spun around, startled. "How the hell—"

"I said stay away from her," the man shouted, hands shaking the end of the pistol. Sharp, blue eyes blazed behind thick spectacles with a crack on the right lens. Strands of dark brown hair parted down the middle hung haphazardly around his forehead.

"Marty!" I cried. "Oh my god!" My eyes widened when I realized he had a gun in his hand.

Vincent raised his hands in the air and began slowly backstepping further into the living room toward the window. "Calm down. Don't do anything rash."

"Step away from her now." Bandages stretched against his grimace. "I'm not going to let you hurt me or Kristen."

"What are you talking about?" Vincent said, eyes narrowed, his hands still in the air. "You're the one with the gun."

Marty hurried over to me. He wrapped his fingers around my wrist and tugged me to him, while keeping the gun trained on Vincent.

"Where are your goons? Are they in the building?"

Vincent paused. He looked at Marty's hand around me then back at Marty. "They're right across the hall. You fire that gun, they'll hear it and come out armed."

Marty closed the door behind him with his foot. "I know you're lying—like always—but just in case." He released my hand, turning the deadbolt and hooking the chain, locking us in with him. He reached into his back pocket and threw a silver chain at Vincent's feet. "Cuff yourself to the radiator."

"Marty, put down the gun! This is crazy," I cried. My pulse was racing against my chest. Blood roared in my ears, drowning out the thoughts screaming in my mind to escape. I wanted to run but had nowhere to go. No, no, no. This couldn't be happening. I was just supposed to talk to Vincent about my pregnancy.

He turned to me, expression softening. "I'm sorry Kristen, I didn't want to have to do this. But he gave me no choice. Please don't be afraid, I'm not going to hurt you. I'm here to protect you."

"Protect me?" I blurted in disbelief, my breaths coming fast and shallow.

Marty tightened his grip on the gun aimed at Vincent's chest then cocked it. The audible click sent a deathly shiver through me. "I'm not going to ask again. Cuff yourself to the radiator, asshole. Do it."

Vincent twisted his head, spotting the cast iron array of pipes behind him situated below the window. "Okay. Okay." He managed to keep his voice even but his movements lacked their usual ease. He slowly bent down keeping both palms open and in front of him. "I'm doing what you asked. Don't shoot." He brought one hand down and picked up the handcuffs, keeping his eyes trained on Marty—and more importantly, the gun in his hand.

I stared. Stunned. Terrified. I was too scared to move as I watched the events unfolding before my eyes.

There was a click. Vincent had cuffed one of his hands to the radiator.

"This is crazy!" I cried.

"Please, Kristen," Marty said calmly. "Give me a chance to explain. I promise we'll get through this."

Chapter Seven

Marty directed me to take a seat on the couch. Tears beginning to blur my vision and my legs unsteady, I nearly stumbled into the coffee table as I silently complied.

"Stay there." His words were calm but they felt like a threat.

Seated, I watched Vincent carefully as Marty approached him, gun in hand. Vincent remained standing on firm legs. He wasn't shaking like I was but his dark eyes were wide and focused. A visibly beating vein along his forehead hinted at the adrenaline pumping through his system. It wasn't supposed to happen like this, I was just supposed to have a conversation with Vincent.

Vincent's free hand twitched. Marty took a step forward, aiming the weapon at Vincent's chest. Marty was close enough for Vincent to sock him across the face or reach for the gun in Marty's outstretched hand. Images of heroic scenarios raced through my mind like scenes from an action movie. My fingers clenched against the cushion of the couch. I was gripped by dread that Vincent would actually try something risky—and fail.

Both men stood facing one another, exchanging fierce stares, neither of them blinking. The moment wouldn't last forever. Someone was going to make a move.

Vincent's body tensed. He swallowed hard. His hand curled into a fist by his side. He glanced at me.

No, don't Vincent! I pleaded with my eyes, unable to find my voice.

Vincent returned his gaze to Marty.

Marty raised the gun and pressed the nozzle into Vincent's forehead. "Get on your knees."

"Don't hurt him! Please!" I pleaded desperately, cupping my hands against my face. I was going to watch Marty shoot Vincent in the head and I was powerless to do anything. My eyes pricked. Tears streamed down my cheeks.

"Please, keep quiet Kristen," Marty said, his tone barely concealing his anger. He kept his eyes trained on Vincent.

Marty reached behind his back and produced another set of handcuffs. He snapped one end around Vincent's free hand and the other end around a different pipe on the radiator, ensuring Vincent wouldn't be able to reach for something to throw or a cell phone to call.

"If you try to get out or if your team comes barging in, I'm going to put a bullet through your head. Understand?"

Vincent eyed him sternly.

Marty grabbed his hair and yanked his head back hard. "I asked you a question, you piece of shit. Do you understand?"

"Yes," Vincent groaned through clenched teeth.

"Good." Marty jerked Vincent's head down, making him wince in pain, then released his hair.

Marty returned to the couch, taking a seat beside me. I shifted away, pressing myself against the armrest and curling my legs into my chest.

"Don't hurt her," Vincent said, lifting his head back up. "This is between you and me. I'm the one who punched you, not her."

"Shut the fuck up. Sit still and be quiet. This is all about me and Kristen. There's no way I'd hurt her. If you want to keep talking, I'm not against hurting you though. God knows you deserve it."

Marty turned to me. "Kristen, I'm so sorry it's come to this." He placed his hand on my shoulder.

The sensation made me hug myself tighter. "Please put the gun down," I said, tears wetting the denim covering my knees. "You're scaring me."

He carefully put the gun down on the coffee table. It was out of his hand but not out of his reach.

"Calm down, babe. Breathe. Tell me you're okay. Please."

I tried my best to calm my nerves, taking deep breaths and hugging myself tightly. "What do you want?"

"Kristen, you have to understand. I wouldn't be doing this if there was any other way."

"Marty, you have a gun. You can't have a good reason for this."

"It wouldn't have come to this if that asshole hadn't beaten the hell out of me." He pointed at Vincent. "I have to protect myself. And you. I need to talk to you."

"Okay," I muttered, lips quivering. I kept my eyes on Vincent, trying to find hope in him. Vincent was returning my gaze, nodding slightly, silently instructing me to stay calm. "I'm listening."

"Please, look at me. Don't be scared," Marty said.

I reluctantly turned my gaze toward him. The bandages covering what used to be a handsome face made him look menacing.

"That's better. Are you okay?"

"Yes," I lied, a tear running down my cheek.

"I need you to hear me out. I'm not going to hurt you." He studied me for a moment, ensuring I gave him my full attention. "This isn't easy for me to say, Kristen." He sighed deeply. "My life's been complete shit since you left me."

Not knowing how to respond, I nodded silently.

"It was so sudden. Why did you leave like that? I know what I did was wrong but you didn't even break up with me properly. After two years together, it was just poof. Gone. How could you do that to me?"

I swallowed hard, hoping my answer wouldn't make him angrier. "Marty, you hurt me. I was afraid."

"We've been off and on before. I thought this was just another hurdle for us to overcome. I didn't know you'd react that way. You'd always been so patient and understanding. Do you know what it's like to have the love of your life just disappear from your world? I was heartbroken. When I went to your apartment in Boston, you were gone. But most of your things were still there. I thought you'd come back for them. I waited for you. Days. Weeks. I slept on your couch, didn't go to work. I called you, sent you messages. You didn't answer any of them."

He studied me for my reaction. I remained silent, sniffling.

"You ran. It took me a while to come to terms with it but when I realized what had happened, I felt horrible. Like I was abandoned. Do you understand how that feels?"

"I'm sorry you've gone through a rough patch."

"I fell apart, Kristen. You know my job as an investment banker? I got fired because I stopped showing up. Then I couldn't get another job. Nobody would hire me. I was too depressed to even care. It wasn't long before I stopped trying. Know what I do now? Or at least what I did until a month ago."

"What?"

"I worked at a McDonalds. That's what it came to after nearly two years of taking odd jobs since you left me. I kept getting fired. My coworkers would always make fun of me. They'd laugh at me. 'Look at the Harvard boy. He's no better than us.' It made me so angry. I was just trying to do my job like everyone else but they thought I believed I was better than them. Which wasn't true! It made me lose my temper."

"That sounds terrible." As much as I hated Marty for hurting me, it didn't make me feel good to hear about how rough his life had been the past two years.

"Yeah, I don't understand why people have to be such shitheads. I try so hard to be a good person but people don't see that. They look at me like I'm rotten when it's them. They're the bad ones. Judging me. Accusing me of things that aren't true. I know I make mistakes but really I'm a good person. You know that, right? Can you ever forgive me for what I did to you?"

"I don't know, Marty. You hurt me very badly."

"I feel awful about it all. There's not a day that goes by that I don't regret what I did to you."

"Okay," I said. "Is that what this is all about? You just want my forgiveness?"

"That's part of it. You mean so much to me. The other part is that I love you, Kristen. I've said it to you before and I meant it. I'll never stop loving you. I need to know how you feel. Do you still have feelings for me?"

"How can you ask me that when you just broke into my apartment with a gun?"

"I told you, I had no choice. It's that fucker's fault. Vincent." He turned to Vincent. "I know who you are. Billionaire, playboy, CEO of Sandworks—Vincent Sorenson." Marty returned his attention to me. "Can't you see he's just using you? He's going to break your heart. He doesn't love you like I do."

"You don't know anything about me," Vincent growled. "I'd never hurt Kristen like you did. You're a monster."

"Look at my face," Marty said to me. He unwrapped his bandages, revealing black and blue swollen skin. "You know who did this? Tell me who's the real monster."

I shook my head. "You're upset, Marty. Even so, you've never gone this far before. Have you been taking your meds or seeing the psychiatrist?"

"I want to but I can't afford those things. They're too expensive."

"Can't your family help you?"

"Not really. You already know I dropped out of law school. That pissed my dad off. When I refused to return to law school, he disowned me. My mom tried to talk some sense into him, but she ended up killing herself last month by taking too many sleeping pills."

My stomach dropped. His mom had been a person with serious issues, but any suicide was a sad situation. "Oh my god."

"Yeah." He paused, his eyes beginning to water. He turned his head, blinked away tears then returned his gaze to me. "It made me realize I need you, Kristen. My life's a mess without you. You're my rock. I can't keep going on without knowing if my only chance at happiness is still out there for me. Can't you see how much I care about you?"

I began to play with my necklace as if I'd just discovered I was wearing it. "This isn't right, Marty."

"Let me see your hand."

The image of Marty twisting my finger flashed through my mind. "W-What are you going to do?" I dropped my hand back down and began to hug my knees again instinctively.

He shifted his seat closer to me, backing me against the armrest of the couch. Leaning over, he reached for my hand and gently pulled my arm away my knees. He brought my pinky up to his lips and kissed it tenderly. I felt like I was going to throw up.

Vincent struggled against his cuffs. "Good lord man, what are you doing? Kristen, he's manipulating you. You have nothing to feel guilty about. He's the one who should feel guilty."

"Stay out of this," Marty spat.

"You make me sick," Vincent said. "Look at yourself, using a sob story to keep Kristen attached to you."

Marty picked up the gun and aimed it at Vincent. "I said stay out of this."

"Marty don't! Put the gun down!"

Marty huffed a few times then relaxed. "He's trying to brainwash you, Kristen. Can't you see that? I don't blame you for what happened, and I'm not trying to guilt trip you. It's not your fault. You're just like me."

"What are you talking about?" I asked, frustrated and scared.

"Think about it, Kris. You ran away from me. From us. You have to admit that's not normal. You should've talked to me. We could've worked things out like we always do. That's what couples do. They work things out together." He kissed my hand again. "I have a theory. And please bear with me on this. Remember how we found out I had borderline personality disorder? Well, I did a lot of research and even talked to Dr. Perkins about this. We think you might have an anxiety disorder."

My head swirled. "What?"

"You're afraid of the unknown, of taking risks, of failing. Remember the anxiety you would get before tests?" Marty chuckled brightly. "I would massage your shoulders for half an hour before the exam then hold you after you finished because you thought you bombed it."

"I don't have an anxiety disorder."

Marty rubbed the back of my shoulder. His eyes were warm and his voice was light-hearted. "Come on, Kris. Don't be so stubborn. It's better if you admit it because then we can do something about it."

I remembered how I had suffered from test anxiety numerous times back in college. Marty had been there to comfort me. Maybe I did have a problem. I ran away from Marty. I ran away from Vincent at the restaurant. I basically ran away from my parents. I was thinking about running away from having my baby. I was afraid of taking risks, afraid of the consequences, afraid of getting hurt, of failing. Riley had said so. Vincent had made me aware of it as well. Now Marty was saying the same thing.

Even with all that, he had no right to try and diagnose me. "No, Marty. Don't tell me I have a problem."

"Shh, shh. I know it's hard to admit. I had trouble admitting I had a problem myself: But it's okay, Kris. I get it now. I understand why you ran away. I just want to help you."

"You seem to be forgetting you invaded your her apartment with a gun," Vincent said, struggling against his restraints.

"You don't understand!" Marty cried. He turned to me. "How can you be falling for this guy, Kristen?"

"You don't know anything about him," I said.

Marty threw his hands up in frustration. "I know he's a smooth-talking player who thinks you're the flavor of the month."

His words hurt me. Although Vincent and I had resolved the miscommunication over Ariel Diamond, the issue had still been lingering on my mind. "Why do you keep saying that?"

"'I have some ideas for some new positions we could take at our next meeting'; 'If you're touching yourself right now, it's only a fraction of the pleasure I'd give you'. Give me a break. He's a douchebag. Just like those frat guys we used to make fun of in college—the ones with baseball caps turned backward and popped-collars. I know how smart you are Kristen. That's why I'm surprised you've been falling for this guy's bullshit."

Hearing Marty recite bits of private conversation between me and Vincent made the blood drain from my face. "How did you know about those things? How did you see the text messages he sent me?"

Marty sighed. "Your phone. Remember I have access to it? I can see your texts and hear your conversations."

"What the hell are you talking about? I never remember agreeing to that."

"Yes, you did. We said we would share passwords. You use the same password for your email as you do for your phone." Seeing my phone resting on the coffee table, he picked it up, tapped at it a few times, then showed me he'd passed the security input to reach the home screen. He smiled. "The word of the day is: waddles. You changed your password on your email and Facebook accounts but I guess you forgot to do it for your phone. You have an app that lets me access your phone through the internet. It's how I've known where you've been all this time."

"What the fuck," I said, shocked at the invasion of my privacy. The signs had been there. Repeated warnings from my service provider about going over my data limit. My phone sometimes randomly turning on at night. He'd been watching me all this time.

"This is so twisted," Vincent said. "You've been stalking her. That's how you knew I was coming over here."

"And you don't think it's twisted putting a tracker on my car? Hiring goons to live in the apartment next door. You're the monster here. What's sick is how you're brainwashing Kristen with your charm!"

"Wait," I said, still reeling. "If you knew where I was, why did you wait two years before showing up at my doorstep?"

Marty's eyes became tender. "I was afraid. I didn't feel like I deserved to see you after what I did to you. I thought you'd come back to me on your own when you were ready. I thought I could be a better man by then and we would be a stronger couple. But things didn't go the way I planned."

I tossed my hands up in the air. "You're not making any sense."

"You were going through a phase. You needed to date other guys and then eventually you'd realize we were meant to be together. That's fine. I'm patient. You dated a few guys but it never got far. It was just a matter of time before you came back. But you went further with Vincent. I was afraid for you. Can't you see why I had to step in? Vincent is bad news."

"You know nothing about me," Vincent said.

"I know you're a charmer. You're a CEO who doesn't have time for personal relationships, never mind giving Kristen the kind of love she deserves. You're just like my dad—wealthy, selfish, egotistical; only thinks about his business. He made my mom so miserable she killed herself. I'll be damned if I let Kristen end up like that."

"I'm not your dad. I'm nothing like your dad. Or you. What the hell's the matter with you?"

"Ask yourself. Who beats someone up like this?" Marty pointed at his face.

"Someone who hates men who abuse women," Vincent growled.

"Don't call me an abuser. It was one time. I have a disorder for god's sake, what's your excuse for what you did?"

"I know guys like you. My sister dated one. You're a piece of shit abuser who doesn't deserve sympathy."

"You know nothing about me! Calling me an abuser is bullshit. I hurt Kristen a little bit one time, and I feel awful about it. You have no right to beat me to a fucking pulp when I try to apologize to her."

"Marty," I said softly. "Vincent and I talked about that. But it doesn't justify you coming into my apartment with a gun."

"Kristen, I told you, I didn't want to do this! What else can I do?"

"Take some fucking responsibility for your actions!" Vincent yelled.

"That's what I'm doing now. I'm protecting her from you."

"You're ruining Kristen's life! If you really care about her, you'd leave her the fuck alone."

"You think I like doing this? This is all because of you."

"You're pathetic," Vincent spat.

"You want to see who's pathetic? I'll show you." Gun in hand, Marty stood up and stomped toward Vincent.

"Marty, no!" I screamed.

Chapter Eight

Marty stood in front of Vincent menacingly. Vincent looked up at him with defiance.

"Let's see how you like it," Marty said. "Kris, turn away. I don't want you to see this."

Marty balled up his fist and punched Vincent across the face.

"Stop Marty!" I screamed.

"Not so easy to beat me up when you don't have your goon squad to hold me down, huh?" he sneered.

Vincent tried to shake off the blow but it was clear he was in pain.

"You don't really care about her. You don't love her like I do," Marty said.

Marty landed another punch to Vincent's face and I shrieked. Vincent didn't protest but his nose began to bleed.

"Admit you don't really care about Kristen." Marty punched Vincent in the gut, knocking the wind from his lungs. "Show her I'm right."

I leaped from the couch, my hand around my necklace. "Stop it Marty! You proved your point. You got your revenge. You don't need to hurt him anymore."

Marty wrinkled his brows. "What's that around your neck, Kristen?"

Oh no. I'd planned on macing him but hesitated because he still had the pistol in his hand.

"Don't touch her!" Vincent shouted hoarsely, straining against his cuffs. He was still trying to catch his breath.

Marty hurried over to me and ripped the necklace off. "He gave you this, didn't he? To buy your affection." Marty examined the heart-shaped pendant. He squeezed it between his thumb and forefinger and liquid squirted out from the bottom onto the carpet. "What the hell? What is this thing?"

I could feel my heart beating through my chest. The one chance I had of getting out of this mess was gone.

He brought his finger up to his nose to sniff then he touched the pad to the tip of his tongue and grimaced. "Is this like pepper spray or something?"

I shook my head, horrified.

"You meant to use this on me didn't you? He made you wear this." Marty went back to Vincent. "Trying to turn her against me? Making me out to be some kind of monster? Let's see how you like being treated like that."

Marty squeezed the pendant and squirted fluid into Vincent's face. Vincent closed his eyes and tried to turn away but it got all over his face.

"Oh god!" I cried.

Vincent didn't cry out in pain. He kept his eyes closed but his jaw was clenched tightly. I could only imagine how bad his eyes were burning right now.

"Say that you don't really care about Kristen. Say it and I'll stop."

"Please, Vincent," I pleaded. "Just do what he wants. I don't want you getting hurt anymore."

Vincent hung his head, panting. He tried wiping off the mace with his sleeve and managed to get enough off to crack open his eyes. "I don't care about Kristen," he murmured, blood dripping from his lip.

Even though I asked him to say it, and the circumstances were extreme, the words hurt more than I anticipated.

Marty grinned wickedly. "That's what I thought." He turned to me. "See, Kris? If I hadn't done this, you would've never known what a liar he really is. See how I'm protecting you?"

"You think you've proven something?" Vincent growled, commanding Marty's attention once again. Still on his knees, he threw his shoulders back and brought his head up, his posture like a soldier's. "My feelings for her go beyond caring. I love her."

Marty became furious. He socked Vincent across the face again. The force of the blow made Vincent turn his head and I could see his eyes were red from the mace.

"No you don't. Say it again. I dare you."

Vincent gazed at me. Both his eyes were bloodshot and one was already swelling from Marty's blows. He looked miserable—a man on the verge of dying. "Look at me Kristen. This might be my last chance to say this."

My breath stopped. My heart pounded in my ears.

"I've felt this way for a while. I knew it was just attraction at first. But after taking you to my island, I realized it was more. So much more. I love you, Kristen. I mean truly love you. Not obsession. Not lust. Not selfish possession. Not some kind of blind idealism. Not some sick, twisted version of love—but the real thing. One with eyes open. One with respect. One that never underestimates the hardships to its existence, never takes the other person for granted. The only kind of love there really is."

"Vincent, no!" Tears streamed down my face.

Marty punched Vincent in the face harder than before. Then Marty kicked him in the stomach. "I warned you!"

"I love you, Kristen," Vincent choked.

"Stop saying that. You're a liar!" Marty kicked Vincent again.

"Please, don't say it again," I sobbed.

"I lo—"

Marty pistol-whipped Vincent on the side of the head. "Don't try to act like you're the hero and I'm the villain. Don't forget you're the one who started this."

"No," Vincent panted, his voice barely above a whisper. "You started it when you hurt her." Every word was strained and seemed to require all his energy just to pronounce.

"How can you even say you love her?" Marty said, flabbergasted. "You barely even spend time with her. You're a fucking hypocrite."

"That'll change . . ." Vincent was visibly struggling to hold his head up. Most of his face was swelling and bleeding now but his eyes were burning with intensity. "It'll work."

"You've only been with her for two months. I was with her for two years!"

"You took her for granted . . . You didn't appreciate her. She's unlike anybody . . . I cherish every moment."

"No you don't. You won't settle down. All you care about is money and excitement. How can you even pretend to be serious about what you're saying?"

". . . We'll settle down when the time is right. For both of us."

Marty threw up his hands, frustrated. "You're going to be a terrible father to Kristen's baby. You're too busy. You wouldn't be there like I would."

No. Marty didn't just say that. He didn't just tell Vincent about the baby. How did he even know about that? Was it from my text messages with Riley about the pregnancy?

"Baby . . .?" Vincent struggled.

"You didn't even know Kristen was pregnant? What a piece of work you are."

Vincent summoned the strength to turn his head in my direction. "Is it true?"

Tears streamed down my face. "It wasn't supposed to come out like this. I wanted to tell you. That's why I called you over."

Vincent's eyes locked with mine. Tears ran down his cheeks.

The sadness in his gaze hurt more than anything I could've imagined. The image of his dark eyes filled with tears ripped through my heart like a bullet.

Chapter Nine

Vincent

One week prior

"So, Vincent . . ."

I knew that tone.

"Tell me more about Kristen," Giselle said as she did some preliminary tidying in the kitchen before Brady's birthday party officially ended.

"She's a very capable analyst recently promoted to wealth manager." I fingered a trace of blue frosting in a nearby bowl, tasted it, then chased it down with a gulp of orange soda. It was delicious. I made a mental note to caution Brady about drinking too much of this stuff. But damn did it taste good to have some every once in a while.

"And . . .?"

". . . And she's funny and caring." *She's also one hell of a minx in the sack*, I thought. Just the thought of her lips wrapping around my cock made me instantly hard even in the most awkward of situations: during business meetings, presentations, even if this conversation. I decided it was better to keep that to myself.

"This is the first time you've let me meet one of your girlfriends and that's the best you can give me? I'm disappointed. Here I thought she was something special."

You don't know how special she is. My mind slipped back to the first time Kristen and I met. Pinching my nipple in that business meeting? I remember thinking in that moment—as her chest was pressed against mine—that she was either the stupidest girl ever or the smartest. Special, for sure. She had quite the set of balls on her. I smiled, suppressing a laugh at the thought.

It wasn't until we started dating that I realized how brave and strong she is—especially with what she'd been through, being in an abusive relationship like Giselle had. It made my blood boil to imagine the silent suffering Kristen endured because of her ex.

"I never said she wasn't."

Giselle shot me a knowing look. "All right, fine. Don't want to tell your sis too much about your love life. I know, I get it. I'm not a gossiping housewife you know. At least not yet anyway."

"You started picking up knitting. I'm not willing to take that risk."

She smiled. "Brady needs sweaters made from love. A boy can't live on trains alone."

"We can agree to disagree on that point," I teased.

Giselle sighed. "You're so fond of Brady. When are you going to have your own kid to spoil?"

I sputtered on my drink.

Kids were something I wanted badly, but it was too early in the relationship to discuss it. It was something I'd hoped for ever since Brady had been born. What I saw in him was what I'd been missing: something worth making money for. Something that made me think beyond the present. Long after I was done risking my life stupidly and working day and night on my company, he would be there, growing and living as I had. I wanted that.

Recovering, I responded, "When I'm with the right person. When the time is right for both of us."

"Mmhmm. I'm not dumb, Vincent. I know you brought her over here for a reason. Maybe to evaluate her reaction around kids?"

Damn, Giselle was clever. I looked around the kitchen, making sure Kristen wasn't within earshot. I could hear her playing with Brady and the other kids in the den. The sound of her laughing and making loud choo choo noises along with the kids made me feel warm and fuzzy.

I lowered my voice. "It's too soon to talk about. Kristen and I have only been dating for two months."

"I know. And yet you've brought her to meet me when you haven't let me meet your other girlfriends. I know you've been in longer relationships than that."

"Those weren't serious."

"Okay. And this one is? Despite being shorter?"

"Quality over quantity. As far as seriousness, it is on my end but we've had some rough patches recently."

"I think she's very serious about you."

"Why do you say that? You guys only talked for a few minutes."

"She seemed very interested in hearing about what I had to say about you."

"Uh . . . what did you tell her?"

"Nothing scandalous." Giselle smiled. "I told her about Mom and Dad and how you changed after that happened."

"How did she react?"

"She seemed very interested in your story."

"Makes sense considering we're dating."

"It's more than that. I think she's really into you, Vincent. I can't put my finger on it but call it woman's intuition. She's probably already thinking about taking things further."

"Let's hope so."

Chapter Ten

Kristen

Seeing the tears from Vincent's eyes made me want to die. He wasn't happy about hearing I was pregnant with his child; he was torn. The tears from his eyes and the pained expression on his face said as much. I thought about rushing Marty. I could try to tackle him out the window. Or wrestling the gun out of his hand. He'd probably end up shooting me but fine, let him shoot me.

Vincent broke his gaze from mine. He drooped his head and his body went limp in his restraints.

Was he dead? Oh god no.

"Stop this Marty! He needs to go to the hospital!"

Marty turned away from Vincent to face me. He started walking toward me with fists clenched. "Why didn't you say that when he was beating me up?"

"I tried! I stopped Vincent from hitting you. Don't you remember?" Seeing Marty approach me, broke me out of a spell. I suddenly feared for my life again. "Please don't hurt me, Marty."

His face softened. "Hurt you? Why do you think I'd hurt you? I told you. I love you. Do you still love me? You must since you protected me."

"Please, don't. We broke up. Protecting someone doesn't mean you love them."

"Did you love me before?"

"I don't know."

"How could you not know?" he shouted. "All those times together. Everything we shared. I loved you. I still do."

"Marty, our relationship was very rocky. We were breaking up and getting back together constantly at the end. I'm still trying to figure out what my emotions were like at that time."

He shook his head. "Do you love him?" he asked frantically. "Do you love Vincent?"

"I don't know."

"Yes or no, Kristen."

I recalled the sad look in Vincent's eyes. It didn't matter anymore. Nothing mattered. I thought I'd escaped Marty but he had known where I was the whole time. I lost Vincent. I was going to lose my job. I was going to lose my life. I was going to lose my baby.

"Yes! I do love Vincent."

His features hardened into a scowl. "You don't mean that."

"I do," I said, mustering up my remaining strength. "I truly love Vincent. I don't care what you say, Marty. Threaten me all you want. I don't love you."

Marty ran a hand through his hair, staining it with the blood on his fist. Vincent's blood. "You're so frustrating, Kristen. You know me. You know how I feel about you."

"No I don't. I don't understand you at all," I cried.

"Stop crying. Stop being afraid of me. I can't take it when you do that."

"I don't care."

"It's because you're carrying his child. That's the reason, isn't it?" Marty approached me, backing me into the couch. His eyes were on my stomach.

"No, don't come near me." I stuck out my hands and feet, trying to shove him away.

"You can't keep me away." His eyes were still on my stomach.

"Don't hurt my baby!"

"You're making me angry, Kristen. You already know you don't want to make me angry."

A loud crack sounded. Where did it come from? It sounded like a wooden plank snapping. Was the couch about to break?

"Marty, no!"

Marty balled his fist.

"Somebody help!" I screamed as loudly as I could.

"Shut your mouth, Kristen. You're out of your mind."

Another loud crack.

Marty raised his fist. I crossed my arms to shield my body, hoping that the flesh and bones in my limbs would prove sturdier than an apartment wall. He was going to punch my stomach. He was going to punch the baby.

"Forgive me, Kristen. I wouldn't do it if I didn't have to."

In a blur, Marty vanished behind the couch. I sat up, realizing someone had tackled him.

"Vincent!" I screamed.

How had he gotten out of the handcuffs?

I leaped from the couch to see Marty and Vincent rolling into the kitchen and crashing into the oven. The force from the impact shook the stovetop and the hot water I'd been boiling in a saucepan for tea tipped and poured over Marty's head.

Marty screamed and frantically swiped at his face with his hands. His face was steaming.

Vincent was groaning and rubbing his head with the heel of his palm. His hands were mangled, his thumbs twisted inward. That's when I realized what happened.

The two loud cracking sounds I heard were from Vincent breaking his own thumbs to escape his handcuffs.

I rushed over to Vincent to try to help him up. He was dazed and couldn't stand up on his own. I hooked my arms beneath his shoulders and tried to drag him to the apartment door but it was difficult to move him. *He's so damn heavy.* I thought about escaping just by myself but I knew I couldn't leave Vincent alone with Marty. Not like this. By the time I came back with the police, Vincent would probably be dead.

Marty blindly reached in front of him, knocking over a jar of sugar and a spice rack on the kitchen counter. White dust and parsley spilled across the counter and the kitchen tile. I'd dragged Vincent a foot when Marty found a towel hanging from the oven. He wiped his face vigorously and opened his eyes.

Before I could react, Marty lunged at us, landing on top of Vincent. I fell backward and smashed into a kitchen table chair.

"You bastard!" Marty cried as he began wailing on Vincent.

Vincent snapped out of his daze and raised his arms to shield his face, shifting his head from side to side to avoid a direct blow.

Frantic, I stumbled to my feet and picked up the kitchen chair with both hands, raising it over my head. Marty leaped from Vincent and rushed me. He swatted the chair out of my hands, making it crash across the kitchen table into the corner. "Don't fight me, Kristen!" he shouted. "I don't want to hurt you." Then he shoved me away. I toppled over the coat rack and into the pile of shoes.

Sprawled over a bed of flats and heels, I spotted the a silver object lying beside the couch. *The pistol.* It must've flown out of Marty's hand when Vincent tackled him. Crawling on my hands and knees across the sea of footwear, I neared the couch and reached for the gun.

The sound of a punch landing on flesh and the sound of a male voice groaning in pain made me realize Marty had mounted Vincent again and was attacking him.

I picked up the gun with shaky hands.

"Stop it or I'll shoot!" I screamed.

Marty continued pounding and shouting at Vincent. He wasn't listening.

"I said stop!" I shook the gun in their direction, but neither of them seemed to hear me. I'd never fired a gun before but I knew how to pull a trigger.

Fearing Marty was going to kill Vincent, I fired a round at the kitchen wall. The sound was almost deafening. The force from the recoil was stronger than I'd expected and I staggered backward, tripping over the coffee table and landing on top of it. The glass shattered under my weight. The back of my head hit something hard. Was it the ground? The broken frame of the table? I laid on a bed of broken shards, the air knocked from my lungs.

The last thing I remembered before blacking out was that the unexpected weight of the gun combined with the shakiness of my hands made the barrel shift downward the moment I pulled the trigger.

The gun had been aimed at Vincent and Marty.

Chapter Eleven

Vincent

Six years prior

My fist was throbbing. I successfully fought the urge to look at it, but I knew it was fucked up from how bad Jim's face had been. Once he was awake, he was going to have some decisions to make about how to fix his features. That nose would never be the same.

I held Giselle as she cried in the same living room our parents had once held us. Even though they were gone, it was still our home.

"You're going to be okay," I said. "I'm going to take care of us."

"Vincent, look at your hand! I'm so sorry," Giselle cried.

It killed me to hear her feel guilty about what had happened to her. As much as my fist hurt, I put the pain to the side. "Stop it, Giselle. You don't have to be sorry about anything. What that bastard did to you wasn't your fault."

She shook her head. "I should have handled it myself. I should have gotten out as soon as it started. I don't know how I let it keep happening."

"It's not your fault, and it's over now." I squeezed her tighter as she sobbed into my shoulder. It was over. That was the only thing that mattered at that moment.

"What if he does come back?" she choked out.

My jaw clenched. She didn't want to know the honest answer to that question. "He won't. If he does, I promise you he'll regret it for every second of the rest of his life."

She stopped crying for a moment and pulled back to look at me. "Vincent, you can't always be around. You have your company to worry about."

"I'll find a way. The only purpose of that company is to provide for you and any other family we ever have. If it doesn't make the lives of the people I love better, I might as well sell the damn thing."

She nodded and sobbed again. Her eyes were puffy and red, and her makeup had been smudged everywhere. Seeing her so disheveled and upset made my stomach feel like a bottomless pit.

Finally, she calmed down enough to speak. "Vincent," she said, her voice small. "I have something to show you."

My eyes widened. I wasn't sure how much more I could take. "What's that?"

She rolled up the sleeves of her green sweater. At first I didn't know what I was looking for, but then I saw them: several raised pieces of scar tissue in a neat row, each in various shades of pink.

My vision blurred as tears welled up in my eyes. "What are these?" I asked quietly.

"Cigarettes."

"You don't smoke."

"He did. Does. Whatever." Tears rolled down both her cheeks.

My heart sank as I put together the implication. "He put them out on you?"

She nodded. "In a neat row. Once for every time I pissed him off. So I wouldn't forget."

My mouth fell open at the audacity of what I was hearing. "He's sick. I'm so sorry, Giselle. If I had any idea . . ."

"You didn't," she said. "I guess I'm pretty good at covering up, but I just have to show you now so I feel like I've come totally clean. I've been hiding it for so long.

I blinked and felt a hot tear roll down my cheek. "I'm so sorry."

She looked down. "He said he would kill me if I told anyone."

I snapped my jaw shut and flexed my still aching fist. "He said he would kill you?"

She nodded.

My heart was pounding in my chest as I breathed heavily in and out. Could I kill someone who had threatened to kill my sister? How would I get away with it?

"Don't even think about killing him first," she said, as if reading my mind.

I snapped out of my plotting. She was staring at me with a very serious expression etched into her features.

"I'm not letting my brother become a murderer."

"But if it's him or you—" I started.

"It won't be. It can't be," she said.

I sighed and took her by the shoulders.

"Fine. But know this: you're the only family I have, and I'm going to protect you no matter what. Even if it costs me my life."

Chapter Twelve

Kristen

The world was fuzzy. Hues of brown and white swirled like cream being stirred into coffee. I couldn't make out any details in the forms that swirled in front of me. What had happened to my vision?

My ears were ringing. My body felt like it was being poked by a thousand needles. It hurt to move. I remembered a gun in my hands going off. How long had I been out?

A shadow shifted into view. It grew larger and more defined. The outline was a figure. Someone was approaching me.

I blinked. The picture became sharper. I blinked again then a few more times. I was staring at the ceiling, the fan spinning.

There was a face in the picture. It was still. Eerily still. Staring at me from above. Who was it?

Blue eyes. Brown hair. Thick spectacles.

Marty.

My hearing slowly returned, but Marty vanished from my vision almost as soon as he appeared. I sat up and saw that Vincent was still fighting with him. Vincent barreled into Marty with his shoulder, pushing him back until Marty was cornered against the wall.

Vincent pummeled Marty with his mangled hands but it was clear that Vincent was at a disadvantage. I looked around for the gun but it was nowhere to be found, it must have gotten tossed somewhere around the room in the confusion.

I saw a small hole on the kitchen wall inches from where they had been. *I didn't hit anyone.*

When I looked over at them again, Marty was kneeling on top of Vincent, straddling him and repeatedly punching him in the face. "Take that you piece of shit!"

"No, Marty! Stop . . . please stop Marty . . ." I pleaded, tears streaming uncontrollably down my face. He was going to kill Vincent, the man who loved me, the man that I loved.

Marty ignored me, continuing to hit Vincent. Vincent had his broken hands up, trying to defend his face. He seemed so helpless in that position that it sent another knife of sorrow into me.

"Stop Marty! Please stop!" I sobbed.

Marty looked up at me, chest heaving, fists covered in Vincent's blood. "Stop? Stop?! It's too late to stop Kristen. You made me do this! This is your fault! Look at what you've done!"

This was my fault. My fault. None of this would have happened if Vincent had never met me. I felt sorrow so intense I wanted to vomit. It was because of me that this monster was hurting Vincent. Killing him.

Marty finally got up from Vincent and walked over to the kitchen counter.

I crawled towards Vincent, the room blurry in my vision. When I got to him, I sat down and cradled his head in my lap. He was still breathing. His breath was heavy and ragged but he was still alive.

"Kristen . . ." Vincent groaned.

"It's okay Vincent. I'm so sorry. I'm so sorry. I'm so sorry. I love you Vincent. I love you so much." I chanted, rocking back and forth. Wet droplets fell from my eyes and splashed onto Vincent, leaving streaks in the dried blood caking his face.

When I looked up again, Marty had found the gun. He had it pointed at us.

We were going to die here tonight.

"You brought this on yourself Kristen . . . you didn't even give me a chance . . ."

Vincent was drifting in and out of consciousness. He stirred, pushing himself up until he was sitting upright, putting his body between me and the gun. Even in this state, with his eyes swollen shut, his hands battered and his face bleeding from cuts and swollen from fractures, he wanted to protect me. Vincent wanted to protect me with his last breath even after I had brought this monster into his life.

"I'm sorry Vincent, I'm sorry about the baby, I'm sorry I didn't tell you early. I'm sorry for Marty. I'm sorry for everything."

I wrapped my arms around Vincent, crying onto the back of his shoulder.

"No, Kristen." Vincent coughed. His voice was low and raspy, barely audible. His eyes were half-lidded. His lips were trembling. He was using every ounce of strength left to talk to me.

I leaned my ear to his mouth to hear the faint words riding his shallow breaths. "No. Don't say that Kristen . . . Don't ever apologize to me for those things . . . You didn't do anything wrong . . . I love you Kristen . . . Let's keep the baby . . . I've always wanted a child . . . We'll raise the child together . . . I love you . . . I want to start a family with you."

My heart was shattering. Vincent was confessing to me that he wanted a family together, moments before we were going to die.

He continued, "I'm the one that should be sorry . . . I promised I'd protect you . . . but I failed . . . I'm sorry Kristen . . . Forgive me . . . I . . . " He was losing consciousness again.

Marty stared at us, his eerie blue eyes filled with anger.

I blinked back my tears and took a deep breath.

Goodbye Riley.

Goodbye Mom.

Goodbye Dad.

Goodbye Vincent.

I'll always love you.

The apartment door exploded. A mist of splinters shot through the air, covering my living room.

"POLICE! DROP THE GUN MOTHERFUCKER!"

I blinked and half a dozen officers were fanned out on my right kneeling behind the kitchen wall and the couch, their guns drawn and aimed at Marty.

Before I could feel any relief, I saw the look in Marty's eyes. They were wide and panicked like the eyes of a cornered animal and he still had the gun pointed at us. He hadn't made any motion to surrender.

The cops were shifting around. They were getting antsy. Marty looked back and forth between us and the cops as if he was deciding what to do. I could see the desperation growing in those blue irises.

No. No. We were so close! This wasn't right. Marty was going to shoot Vincent anyway. We were so close. It wasn't fair. It wasn't right. We were so close to being safe, to being happy.

"DROP IT ASSHOLE! THIS IS YOUR LAST WARNING!"

Marty didn't care about getting shot himself. He was going to empty the clip into Vincent and at this distance, he wouldn't miss. I could see the events playing in his mind: he would shoot Vincent then me while the cops shot him down.

I had to try; I had to try one last time to get through to Marty.

I wiped the wetness from my eyes and looked into Marty's face. "No Marty, please . . . Marty you need help . . . Vincent and I . . . we love each other. You and I had something, but that was long ago. You need to get help Marty. Don't take Vincent away from me. Don't take my life away from me. If you ever loved me, if what you said was true about still caring about me, do the right thing. Please Marty, think about what you're doing. You're going to ruin all of our lives."

His brows narrowed. A strange expression crossed his face. Maybe it was a rare moment of lucidity for him or maybe I just imagined it, but it seemed like he suddenly realized what he had become. For a split second, I thought I saw a glimpse of the Marty that I knew years ago. Blue eyes, brown hair, boyish smile.

His arm wavered, then went limp. The gun clattered on the floor.

And then it was over.

Chapter Thirteen

When the ambulances arrived, Vincent had regained a bit of his strength. He insisted on riding to the hospital up front in the same ambulance as me, even though he was in a much worse state than me. The paramedics argued with him for a while, before letting him have his way. They must've figured that this way they would at least get him to the hospital, even if he refused to get there on a stretcher.

I lay in the stretcher as the paramedics fussed over him, wrapping up his hands and flushing his eyes with water.

"Kristen, I meant everything I said before. I love you. If you want to have the baby, I'll be right there with you. It's up to you Kristen, but I love you. I'll be here for you, no matter what you decide."

"Is that what you want Vincent?"

He nodded. His eyes were glistening, I'm not sure if it was from the water the paramedics were rinsing his eyes with or from tears.

"When we were back there and Marty told you about the baby, for a moment, I thought you didn't want the baby," I said.

"I've wanted a child for a while now, Kristen. When you told me, I was so happy. . . but I thought I was about to lose it all. I love you Kristen. If you're ready, I want to start a family with you. Do you want that?"

I struggled to find the words. "I—I love you too Vincent, and I think I do want a family, but I don't know yet. Things have just been so crazy, we should take some time and think about it in case either of us changes our minds."

He gave me his hand, wrapped in medical bandages and I latched onto it. "I won't change my mind Kristen, but you're right. We'll talk about it later. All I care about right now is that you're okay."

I pursed my lips. He was going to make me cry again.
"I'm glad you're okay too, Vincent. I thought I was going
to lose you."

Vincent let out a deep breath and chuckled. "You can't
get rid of me that easily."

His expression turned serious again. "I'm sorry about all
of this Kristen. This was all my fault. Earlier today, when
we were interrupted in the office, it was Kurt and Bernie.
They had come to tell me that they lost track of Marty. I
should have realized that he was more dangerous than
he seemed."

"No Vincent, you didn't know. How could you have
known that Marty would react that way? I didn't even
know. I thought he had changed and got the help he
needed and was recovering. I was wrong about him too."

Vincent growled, "Guys like that don't learn their lesson
until you bury them under six feet of concrete."

"I wouldn't have wanted you to do that Vincent. That
wouldn't have been right. Marty is sick."

He let out a long sigh, "It doesn't matter anymore. Now you're safe and you won't ever have to be afraid of him ever again."

"If you hadn't met me, if I hadn't dragged you into my problems, none of this would've happened. Your hands . . ."

"Don't you dare say that Kristen. If I hadn't met you, my life wouldn't have been whole. I don't regret a single moment I've spent with you. I'd gladly trade my thumbs, my hands or any parts of my body for you Kristen. You're everything to me."

"Did you really mean it when you said you wanted to start a family?"

"I know we haven't been dating for that long Kristen, and I don't know what the future holds, but I know how I feel about you."

"What about your company?"

"They don't need me there all the time. I'll take more time off to be with you. You're more important to me."

"What if . . . what if it doesn't work out?"

"We can't live life based on 'what ifs' Kristen. We'll make it work."

Vincent looked around the ambulance and then raised an eyebrow at me, it looked almost comical on his swollen face. "So . . . 'waddles' was your phone password huh?"

I half-laughed half-sobbed in relief and held on more tightly to his hand. No matter what happened next, we would work through our issues together.

Epilogue

"Ouch."

"Oh, I'm so sorry," I said.

"It's fine. Just try not to put too much pressure there," Vincent said.

He moved his arm out from under me and I stroked it lightly. The cast had come off a month ago, but sometimes it was still sore for him. In addition to breaking his thumbs, Vincent had also fractured his forearm in the fight with Marty.

Marty was prosecuted and locked up. Even though he needed serious help, it was because of his ill-guided actions that Vincent and I were closer together. I wasn't happy about what happened to Marty, but I knew that he would finally be able to get the help he needed in prison.

Sunlight drifted in through the translucent blinds, illuminating small specks of dust floating in the air.

Vincent beamed at me, his eyes still squinty from sleep. We were in his New York penthouse. Though I would have preferred the tranquility of his island, Vincent insisted on being in Manhattan so that we could be close to the New York Presbyterian Hospital. He told me that it had the best neonatal care unit in the world.

I snapped back to the present and Vincent was looking at me with a suggestive look on his face. His cock was out and he was nudging at my entrance.

"Wait, aren't you missing something?" I teased him.

He nuzzled his chin against the side of my face. "Like what?"

The light fuzz on his chin rubbing against me made it difficult not to giggle. "Like a condom. That's how we got here in the first place."

Vincent had proposed to me as soon as we had gotten out of the hospital. We had many serious talks while we were both recovering. Somehow, despite it being against hospital policy, Vincent had gotten us placed in the same recovery room. After the events we had been through, it was pretty clear that we both wanted to raise a child together.

Giselle had visited us a few times with Brady and Rob. She gave me a few tips on making the pregnancy go more smoothly and I appreciated the time I spent with her. She wanted to know the sex of the baby, but we didn't even know—we wanted it to be a surprise. I was looking forward to calling Giselle my sister-in-law.

Vincent lifted his head up and smiled down at me.

"But I like where we are now."

"You're not worried about how our lives will change with a baby in the picture?"

He propped his head up with his other arm, his expression turning serious. "I'm excited. In fact, I'm going to come inside you and we're going to make twins."

I laughed. "I hate to burst your bubble but that's not how it works."

"It might be improbable but we've beaten the odds before." Vincent kissed my round belly before laying the side of his head against my chest.

"So you're going to break the rules of biology now?"

I pushed myself up until I was propped against the headboard. Vincent shifted and grimaced as he put his weight on his injured arm.

"Maybe when I get my full strength back, we'll give it a shot."

After we had talked in the hospital, we decided that it would be best if I left my job at Waterbridge-Howser and helped Vincent manage his wealth until I gave birth. With the way things had been going at Waterbridge-Howser, I would've been forced out sooner or later, and I would always have to sleep with one eye open, knowing that Richard had it out for me.

Our plan was that Vincent would help me establish my own wealth management firm afterward. I wasn't sure about it at first, but he'd convinced me that I had all the skills I needed and he had the connections to get me up on my feet. Vincent started delegating a lot of his work in order to spend more time with me, and in preparation for taking care of the baby. He also cut out the riskier aspects of his love of extreme sports, though he still enjoyed surfing occasionally.

I'd moved out of my place with Riley and in with Vincent. Riley had a few blush-worthy comments about sex during a pregnancy, but she was overjoyed for us and insisted on being involved in planning the wedding.

I'd finally called my parents and invited them to the wedding that was happening six months from now. It was still awkward, but they'd seemed happy for me. I don't know if I will ever be close with them, but at least they could still be a small part of my life.

"Not feeling so invincible anymore huh Mr. Risk-Taker?" It felt good to be like this, just lounging around and teasing each other.

"I feel great. How do you feel?"

"I don't know, maybe you can make me feel even better," I said smiling.

"Insatiable." Vincent kissed me and rolled me onto my back. "That's the woman I love."

"The heart wants what the heart wants."

It turned out Vincent had been right all along. *Nothing worth pursuing comes without risk*. I took a risk in a bar in South Africa with deadly spiders. I took a risk dating Vincent when it could have cost me my job. And I took a risk trusting Vincent, Mr. Trouble-At-First-Glance, when I was afraid nothing good would come of it.

Vincent held me tightly and I relaxed into his arms as two—no—three hearts beat together. Everything my heart ever wanted was right here with me.

Thank you for reading!

If you could spare a moment to leave a review it would be much appreciated.

Reviews help new readers find my books and decide if it's right for them. It also provides valuable feedback for my writing!

Sign up for my mailing list to find out when my next book is released!

http://eepurl.com/sH7wn

Made in the USA
Lexington, KY
28 April 2014